A VISION OF HELL

Borgo Press Books by BRIAN STABLEFORD

A VISION OF HELL

THE REALMS OF TARTARUS, BOOK TWO

BRIAN STABLEFORD

THE BORGO PRESS

MMXII

A VISION OF HELL

FIRST BORGO PRESS EDITION

Published by Wildside Press LLC

www.wildsidebooks.com

ACKNOWLEDGMENTS

I am greatly obliged to Heather Datta for her great kindness and consummate efficiency in scanning the text of the first edition of this novel, thus enabling me to get it back into print.

A VISION OF HELL

A VISION OF HELL

1.

Camlak was not unduly sensitive to time. It passed by without dragging his consciousness. It flowed over him in an easy stream. The silence was profound. The Ahrima had gone, but the fires they had left burning were still filling the air with heavy smoke and the stark smell of ashes. There would be a while yet before the fire yielded to the gentle smell of decay and carrion that would bring the scavengers in from the fields, and from the wild land beyond Clauster Ridge.

The Old Man of Stalhelm was hurt, but not badly—at least, not so far as bone and flesh and blood were concerned. The arm which he had broken in the fight with the harrowhound had shattered for a second time, and he knew that this time there would be no mending it. From now on he was a three-limb. But that was little enough. It would not have taken him out of the fight, and saved his life. A blow on the head had done that, without inflicting any lasting damage. His clothing was covered in blood—dry by now—and no doubt he had looked dead enough to the marauders, lying as he was within the star-shadow of the earthen wall, with the mutilated bodies of the honest dead all around him. It was, of course, their blood. Blood they had spilled on to him, so that chance might rule in favor of his continued existence. The principal hurt which he had sustained was the pain of the question: *why?*

He was three times lucky.

First, he had fallen from a light, glancing blow, and sheer exhaustion had sucked him to the ground and hugged him into the crack between earth and earth-wall. Somehow, he had found the strength to suppress his courage. How? The Ahrima were already over the wall and involved in the simple business of slaughter. It was natural that he should have fought with indomitable fury, without any such self-control, or even self-awareness. He should have bounced back from the blow. But he had not. He had sagged, had contained his instincts, had vanished into the black clothes of unconsciousness.

Then, somehow the Ahrima had failed to find him. Or failed to find him alive. The one who had felled him must have been felled in his turn, at the right moment. At precisely the right moment. He must have died very swiftly, spilling his blood with such profligacy that he seemed to have exploded. A combination of chances: a neat riposte of fortune. Too neat.

Lastly, Ermold must have been already dead. The Men Without Souls from Walgo had taken the mask and joined the Ahrima in the assault on Stalhelm. A victory not so much for cowardice as for Ermold's hatred. He had come to kill instead of being slaughtered by the horde. He would die anyway, but he had come to kill first. Had he survived the storming of the wall, he would surely have come to take Camlak's head. A gesture to underline the purpose of it all. For old time's sake. Chance had forbidden him that satisfaction.

Why?

Camlak hurt inside his head. There was a fever in his brain. A fog. He tried to reach down into the depths where his Gray Soul lived, but the way was blocked. Honest pain would have cut through the miasma like a hot spear. No man was denied the company of his Gray Soul in the moment before death, or the moment of bodily crisis. So Camlak believed, with reason. But he was trapped in his glutinous consciousness. He was not going to die. He was alone.

He believed that there had to be an answer to the question: *why?*

But he did not even know what shape such an answer might possess.

2.

The Ahrima had not lingered long once Stalhelm was taken and set afire. There was nothing to stay for. Everything which was truly valuable had been taken by the women who had left for Lehr the moment the Ahrima were sighted and the warning given. Camlak might have been counted lucky even a fourth time, in that the marauders had chosen to move on, but it was not chance which dictated the decision. The Ahrima wanted blood, and a great deal of blood. They had not spilled so much as a mouthful at Walgo, and fully three-fourths of the population of Stalhelm had fled before their advance. They wanted the blood of that three-fourths. They wanted to ride down the women and children who hastened along the road to Lehr. They wanted the plunder of Stalhelm far more than they wanted the rest or the food that was standing in the fields. It was not their way. Once the slaughter of the townspeople was completed... *then* they could think of rest and the licking of wounds and the filling of bellies. At Lehr, or perhaps Opilion, where they might not be expected so soon....

In any case, Camlak would not have claimed luck for the decision which would—almost inevitably—lead to the slaughter of his people. If the Ahrima caught the women and children on the road through Dossal Bog, then Stalhelm was obliterated. What the fire could not do, the sword would accomplish. It was the people that were Stalhelm, and once the people were dead...no Stalhelm. The name would remain, but names mean nothing.

Some of the people would survive. Perhaps some of the warriors had managed to escape the burning village to fight again on the road. In any case, in Dossal Bog there would be ample opportunity to run and to hide. Some of the women, and particularly the children, would escape the Ahrima in the marshland. Some of those would survive the perils of the bog. Some, perhaps, would ultimately return to the blackened ruin that had been their home. But all that counted for very little. Camlak's Stalhelm could not be recovered by a handful of children. Unless the warriors of Lehr came out to cover the retreat of the women, or something delayed the horde on the road, that Stalhelm would be strewn in a gigantic pool of blood all over the road through Dossal Bog.

After that...well, the news would reach Lehr, Opilion, and fly like a freak wind through the north and west of Shairn. If the Shaira could then allow their common fears and needs and causes to overcome their petty quarreling and disputes over land, all Shairn might combine to raise an army and meet the Ahrima in a battle that would cut the horde's strength so hard they would have to run. Even that would only be a beginning. With the heart of Shairn ripped open, its strength expended in a murderous encounter with the Ahrima, the Men Without Souls would move in, raiding the good lands, stealing Shairan land and taking Shairan slaves. After the war of extinction, the war of conquest.... And then....

Harrowhounds would come. The vermin from the dark lands would spill over into the lighted lands of the Children of the Voice. Time and time and time would pass before Shairn became Shairn again. And if the Ahrima were *not* defeated, if no army was joined and the horde was not cut to such dimensions that the towns were safe...then Shairn might follow Stalhelm, and by the time the country lived again it would be something different. Something new.

When Camlak finally came to his feet again he discovered that he was angry with Ermold. He was angry because of Ermold's hate—the blind, unreasoning hate which had made him take the mask and join in the attack on Stalhelm. Camlak saw no reason for that hate, and because there was no reason he was angry. He considered Ermold's taking of the mask a betrayal. Not a betrayal of the Shaira, to whom he owed no loyalty, but a betrayal of reason and of human nature. Walgo should have stood and fought. That was the way. Perhaps there was no difference between the Men Without Souls and the Ahrima but masks, but the masks meant something. They were real. The Men Without Souls had no reason to be something that they were not. They should have fought. Perhaps...perhaps they should have fought *with* Stalhelm, *against* the Ahrima. Was that against nature, too? Camlak thought not. Not against *his* nature. Ermold's nature, on the other hand....

Camlak dismissed the argument from his maddened mind.

He could not think. The anger remained. He could still feel— perhaps too much.

Camlak's house was burning. The bricks were crumbling as the wooden framework and the roof were eaten away. When the fire died there would be nothing left but ash and rubble. In time, dust. Only dust. The smoke was foul, but Camlak managed to suck enough oxygen into his lungs to keep himself conscious and active. Foul air meant little enough to him, or to any child of the Underworld.

Some of the other houses still stood, untouched. Something to come back to, if anyone could come back. Or somewhere for Hellkin to find refuge, somewhere for the Truemen who came from beyond Cudal Canal to establish themselves. Ultimately, the houses would decay, or form the focus for a new community. Either way, the real Stalhelm would be buried, haunted by the living and the dead alike. Nowhere and nowhen. Gone.

Camlak wandered around the dried-up streets, searching out the bodies of the fallen, putting names to the faces and the faceless. He had the vague idea that others might be alive. But there was no one. It pained him to count how few of the bodies were Ahriman. He plucked masks off a few of the fallen, and shattered them by beating them against the cornerstones of houses which remained intact. He did not know why. He might have been searching for Ermold, though there was no real reason. In any case, he could not tell the Men Without Souls from the true Ahrima until he removed the masks. Though there were too few to give his counting satisfaction, there were too many to sort into real and unreal, looking for one filthy face, for no good reason.

He felt guilty because he—the Old Man—should have been the only one singled out to survive (except, perhaps, for those who had run). He was the custodian of the staff. While the Ahrima were crossing the borders of Shairn, he had been taking power from the Star King Yami. Against the odds, against all the accusations, against the feeling of the people, he had established himself. He had fought the harrowhound to earn the right. And now he was Old Man of nothing, but still Old Man. What he felt was a strange kind of loneliness. He felt responsible for what had happened. He wanted to take the burden of guilt for the disaster on to himself. He was the Old Man, and he had earned it. He had earned it the hardest way of all. He felt that he had the right to feel betrayed by the chance which would not let him lie dead with the people—*his* people. They had never learned to trust him. They had never had the chance.

Eventually, he tired of looking at the dead, and he went into one of the untouched houses to change his clothes. The Ahrima had smashed up what they could, but their assault had been cursory—there was no real reward, material or emotional, in destroying inert objects—and he had no difficulty in finding what he needed, and then in preparing himself a meal. What the Ahrima had left was sufficient—in fact, the stripping of the village was more the work of the women than the invaders. The women had taken all that they could carry. Too much. Too much in the way of baubles and cloth. Along with the working tools and the books, the irresistible trivia would make too heavy a burden. The fleeing women might find themselves betrayed by their fondnesses. The road to Lehr would be strewn with things which, after all, had to be thrown away. Would the greed and the delight in possession deliver them into the hands of the Ahrima? Would sound common sense or sheer blind panic have delivered them? There was no way of knowing.

Even when he was rested and fed, clothed and armed, he still hesitated. He went back to wandering amid the dead, finding it impossible to believe that there was no life at all in Stalhelm. But by now there was. The starlings and the crabs were invading in force. Camlak began to kill, shattering the crabs with a stone axe. Against the starlings, he could do nothing. Eventually, he threw away the axe, because there were too many crabs. No matter how many he killed, it would make no difference. They would keep coming until the village could hold no more. No matter how many crabs were killed the Underworld was always as full of them as it could be. It made no sense. Killing them only made him feel worse.

In the end, he had to leave Stalhelm to the scavengers. It was theirs now, and if he stayed he would be one of them. The only question in his mind was the matter of which way to go. Where and why? There was a road to Lehr, a road which might run with blood, and which might take him to his death. For no real reason. On the other hand, there was the Swithering Waste. No road was there, but perhaps some kind of destination. Nita had gone that way, with the man who had no face. Beyond the Waste was the metal wall, and beyond that...if there *was* a beyond. But that way was clouded with doubt no less than the road to Lehr. Whatever choice he made, there would only be more choices, until he was interrupted by death. There was no known way, now that Stalhelm was gone.

Camlak felt the loneliness eating him from within.

He went to find the map which had hung on the wall in the long house. It had been torn down and slashed into three pieces by a sword. He put the pieces together on the long table and adjusted the edges.

Nita would have taken the man without a face and the girl Huldi over the hills called Anarek and Stiver, across the rocks at Scarmoon, and then into the Swithering Waste toward the Great Wall. Camlak tried to form an estimate of how far they would have gone, but the calculation defeated him. He had no way of measuring the time inside his head. If he could catch up with them while they were crossing Scarmoon, it would be easy enough to find them, but in the Waste it would need a miracle.

The Waste was hundreds of miles across, and to the west it stretched to the dead cities and the very borders of the dark-lands—a vast expanse of poisoned shallows and jagged rock, completely overgrown and teeming with vermin—and worse. A death trap. No place to be wandering in search of other travelers. Once Nita was beyond Scarmoon, he would have virtually no chance of meeting her until the Wall. If that were so, then time now was not really of the essence.

In the emotional battle between the father of the child and the Old Man of Stalhelm, the father really had little chance. That was the way love worked in the Underworld, at least in Shairn. Camlak needed to know what had happened to the people. He could not turn his back on the leadership which he had fought so hard to win. He had to know what happened on the road to Lehr, and he had to know by seeing. There was no other way.

From the vantage on top of the skull-gate he could see as far as the canal ridge out toward Walgo but only as far as the hilltops in the southwest. The forested slopes cut off his view of Dossal Bog. The Ahrima and the rogue Truemen were well out of sight by now.

As he went through the skull-gate and turned toward Lehr he reflected that Stalhelm had stood a long time in the farthest reaches of Shairn. By the tally of the gate the people had done well. But he knew that the dead get no credit in the tally of survival, and the contribution of the knitted skulls to the future of the Children of the Voice was purely negative. It was a symbol, not a magical guarantee. Yami's head-taking ways had not, in the end. preserved Stalhelm forever, even if Yami had not lived to see its fall. Yami, as a good leader, had even known precisely when to die. If anyone remembered Stalhelm at all, they would remember Yami, and the brief hour in which Camlak had reigned would be forgotten as the blackest time in the town's history. So much for three times lucky.

Camlak left his home for the first and last time, and went into the Underworld.

3.

The history of the Overworld began, according to the Euchronian Movement, at the close of the second dark age (which they also called the age of psychosis). Naturally enough, there was no one to disagree with them. In point of fact, however, an unbiased observer—Sisyr, perhaps—might have traced the Overworld *mentality* much further back than that. At least a thousand years, and probably two. A devout Euchronian might shrug his shoulders, and point out that an odd millennium or two was little enough compared with the eleven thousand years of the Euchronian Plan (let alone the half a million years the Euchronians were prepared to spend if that were necessary), but a historian would have recognized the flaw in such a comparison of duration. The velocity of history is not uniform. "Progress" (a mythical concept dating back to prehistoric time) is not constant.

However, it was certainly during the second dark age that the Movement was formed and the Plan was born. According to Euchronia, the Movement and the Plan saved the world. No one would disagree with that, either. By Euchronian standards, Euchronia had saved the world. It had discarded the old world and built a new one, on a platform which was mounted over every convenient acre of the old world's land surface.

In the beginning, the Plan had been ludicrous. The Euchronians had accepted that in those days (they denied it now), but they had pointed out with some justice that if ludicrous ambitions were all that were left, they were the only recourse of hope.

Work on the Plan had been underway for several centuries when Sisyr's starship arrived in the solar system. The Euchronians never actually found out *why* Sisyr came to Earth, although they did discover that his arrival at precisely the time when they needed him most was purely fortuitous. Whatever the reason, Sisyr was ready and willing to set it aside in order to provide Euchronia with the technical expertise and the scientific knowledge which they lacked. The margin between failure and success was undoubtedly filled by Sisyr. Without his intervention time would most definitely have run out for the dying Earth. As it was, the assistance of the alien and his home world, though slow to be provided (starships took centuries to cross the interstellar gulf between the two worlds) turned the tide.

Euchronia was suitably grateful to Sisyr, but it also found it very convenient to forget him. The Movement had its pride, and it needed the credit more than he did. Sisyr went into quiet retirement somewhere on Earth, atop one of the mountains which projected its peak into the Overworld. He asked nothing other than a home and a quiet life. The Euchronians presumed that he would die one day and could then be obliterated entirely from the history of the Earth. They were wrong. While thousands of years rolled by, Sisyr showed not the slightest sign of dying. Earthly memories, however, were short, and Sisyr's active contribution to the Plan ended long before the platform was complete and the world rebuilt upon it. The only real reminder of his existence was the fact that two or three times a century a star-ship would land, but the aliens were discreet, and they bothered no one except Sisyr.

The platform was completed in six thousand years. The world in which the Euchronians were destined to live was finally pronounced complete after eleven thousand. The cities were finished, the cybernet which would provide the needs of the community was complete—a gargantuan mechanical beast for the humans to parasitize. The Euchronian Millennium was declared and the people settled down to enjoy it.

They did not know how. They only knew why.

Hundreds of generations of Euchronians had spent their entire lives laboring toward an end they knew they would never see. Billions of lives had been given up absolutely to the ideal of the Plan. For eleven thousand years, the purpose of life in Euchronia had been labor, unselfish and unrewarded: the infinitely protracted process of giving birth to a new existence. And when the birth was achieved....

The purpose of life was lost.

The Planners had anticipated this. They knew that there would have to be a period of adjustment, and they knew that period would be measured in centuries rather than in years. The Utopian potential of Euchronia's Millennium would have to be carefully developed and brought to flower. It would take time and effort. The Planners, with the supreme optimism which had guided their forebears out of a ruined Earth and toward a promised land, led them to believe that it could and would be done. It had to be done—to justify the Plan. But when the Millennium came, they only knew what and why. They did not know how. This time, they could only rely on their own resources. They could not ask Sisyr for help.

The people of Euchronia's Millennium were living in a functionally designed Utopia, but they had problems. They were not Utopians. They were, in a sense, a society of misfits. Empirically maladjusted. The builders of a new world are *ipso facto* ill fitted to live in it. The mother cannot be expected to live the life of the child. Mothers who try destroy their children.

Among the methods adopted by the Planners to facilitate the Plan was the i-minus effect—the chemical control of dreams. I-minus was calculated to exorcize instincts, so that social conditioning—functional social conditioning—might be made one hundred percent effective. It worked. It continued to work after the Millennium, but no one could tell whether the fact that it worked was useful or not. No one could judge the situation well enough to decide whether the effect ought to be continued or not, or even how such a decision might be made. This exemplifies the confusion of the citizens of the Millennium. They were as helpless as newborn children. An infant society. Ignorant, yet not knowing of their ignorance; blind to the contexts of their existence, yet not knowing of their blindness.

The society of Euchronia's Millennium was vulnerable. Its vulnerability was exposed by Carl Magner, who rediscovered the Underworld in his nightmares. (How? There was no way of knowing.) Perhaps the rediscovery of the ruined Earth was the last thing the Euchronians needed. Perhaps, on the other hand, the rediscovery of the Hell which the Plan had left behind was the only way in which the people could come to terms with the Heaven it had built.

Perhaps it would help them to rediscover themselves.

4.

Rafael Heres had to make a statement to the Euchronian Council. The pressure on him had grown, and he knew that the current of opinion which was flowing through the Council was set against him. But it had been so before, and he had survived. Usually he stirred up big enough waves to make countercurrents of his own to drown out the others. He had faith in himself now. He knew that the only significant opposition to him, in the past and the present, was Rypeck. He had always controlled Rypeck, and he was sure that he could hold him now.

He opened his address by telling them that Carl Magner was dead. Some of them already knew, but to most it came as something of a shock. That a man should die was not uncommon, but that a man like Magner should die by assassination beside a public road was a strange and upsetting thing. That fact alone stilled the currents of hostility. It changed the game completely. Almost, if such a thing was conceivable in this day and age, it made it look as if the Magner affair might not be a game at all. (But even in games, pieces lose their lives.)

Heres talked about Magner, who had somehow become so important that the Hegemon of the Euchronian Movement could deliver an obituary for him. Heres talked calmly about Magner's background, and the tone of his voice not only expressed his own sympathy but went out into the multilink to grab sympathy from the listeners. He gave little attention to the tragedies which had marred Magner's life, but simply by numbering them he made certain that everyone appreciated what a hard time the man had had.

A less subtle man might have used the statement to build a case against Magner—to turn his public image into the effigy of a madman, preparatory to burying his memories and his ideas forever. But that was what many of them expected. That was what most of them already believed. Heres knew, as any leader knows, that it is dangerous to confirm what people already know. A leader should always be ahead, moving amid the ideas that people have not yet discovered. Magner's death had changed the game, and Heres wanted to be the one to work out the new rules.

It took Heres a little over an hour to make a martyr out of Magner. Instead of claiming that Magner's experiences had made him mad, the Hegemon suggested that the pain and the anguish had lent Magner a keener insight into life than was possessed by the majority of the carefully cushioned citizens of Euchronia's Millennium. He said, in fact, that Magner had become a visionary—a man who saw beyond the present and the legacies of the past to the realms of possibility and the legacies which ought to be put in hand for the future.

"Before he was killed," said Rafael Heres, "Carl Magner stood at the focus of a controversy which grew around him like a storm. Some of you may have seen the discussion which took place between Magner, Clea Aron and Yvon Emerich on the holographic network last night. The arguments there made only a beginning in searching out the implications of Magner's theories, but they will have served to familiarize many of you with the fundamentals of the problem.

"Carl Magner accused Euchronian society of a crime of omission in that the Movement has, at least since the Millennium, ignored and forgotten the world which still exists beneath us— the surface of the Earth from which our ancestors came. Magner wanted to remind us that the old world, from whose ashes the new one arose, was never totally consumed. He claimed that there are still men in the Underworld, living in the darkness because our world enjoys the sunlight that once was theirs. We know that the sunlight used to be ours too, and some of you would argue that we have merely preserved it while the men on the ground willfully forsook it. That may be, but as Carl Magner has tried to remind us, that was thousands of years ago. The men who live in the Underworld now are not responsible for the decisions of their forefathers.

"I do not think that there can be any possible question about the actions of the Planners in the remote past. No one was denied the chance to make himself part of the Plan, from the moment that the Movement was founded to the moment when the last section of the platform cut off the last rays of sunlight from the last few acres of the derelict surface of the old world. No decision which we make today or in the future will reflect on the choices made in the past by the men of the past. But the situation today is different. Different circumstances call for new decisions—we cannot simply keep echoing the old ones. The Planners of the Euchronian Movement set out to build a world for *us*—their ultimate descendants. They did what they set out to do. We inherited that world, we have it now, and there can be no limit to our gratitude toward those who made it for us. We value this world very highly—it is our life and we guard it as we do our lives. We will continue to do so. We will continue to value and protect our own existence and the manner of that existence.

"Carl Magner asked us to open the doors of our world to the people of the Underworld. This we cannot do. To open our world is to threaten it. But this does not mean that Carl Magner's accusations were untrue.

"We *have* forgotten the Underworld. The people who live in the Underworld today, if people there are, are *not* the people who refused to join the Plan, who made a free choice and chose to live their lives as they would.

"We remember the men who stayed on the ground rather than work for a new world as cowards and traitors, and perhaps we have reason for this. But we must not judge too harshly. It was their right to choose, and it remained their right throughout the centuries when the two worlds were coexistent. How many of us are the descendants of late recruits, who joined the Movement a hundred, or a thousand years after the Plan was first put into operation? We do not know. It makes no difference. It does not matter whether our ancestors in the age of psychosis were committed Euchronians, or the grandfathers of converts. Why should it? How can it?

"I believe that Carl Magner was right to remind us of the world we left behind. I believe he was right to ask us whether there are men on the ground today, and if so, whether we owe them something because we have taken away their sunlight. The Marriage of Heaven and Hell which he suggested is not the right answer, but the question which Magner asked remains the right question.

"The Euchronian ideal—the ideal which built the new world, and which gave us everything that we are and everything that we have—is the principle of working together for the benefit of others. The Planners worked for their children, many generations hence, but how many Planners died childless? How many of the men who worked for our world have no descendants living here? Again, we do not know. Again, what does it matter? For those men, the ideal remained. They still gave their lives to the Plan, if not for their own children, then for the children of their neighbors, and the children of men who lived and worked on the other side of the world.

"The Euchronian Plan was declared complete two centuries ago. We live now in what we are pleased to call the Euchronian Millennium, the world which is our heritage. But can we really call ourselves Euchronians? We work, we live useful lives. But the people *for* whom we work, and to whom we offer our resources, are ourselves. If we are Euchronians, then perhaps we should look beyond ourselves. Perhaps we should look beyond our children and our children's children, whose future, we hope, is secure because of the efforts of the Planners. Perhaps we should remember the Underworld, and ask ourselves whether we might devote something of our effort and endeavor toward doing what even the Planners themselves could not do and did not try. Perhaps, now that we have our world secure in the sky, we should begin to make another new world—another good and safe world, where men can live secure and free lives—out of the surface which languishes beneath our feet.

"We cannot bring the people of the Underworld into our world. But we can help them to rebuild theirs. We can offer them knowledge and supply them with tools and power. We can give them everything that they need to set in motion their own Euchronian Plan, and we can help them to make it successful. We can give them everything...except the sunlight, the Face of Heaven which Carl Magner wanted to give them. But we can supply light instead of sunlight. We can help them to find a different face for *their* Heaven. We owe them that. We must owe them that, at least.

"Members of the Council, I propose that we give our attention, from this moment on, to the making of the new Euchronian Plan."

5.

Heres believed that he had saved the world. Two worlds, in fact. That was—had to be—the perfect solution. The ideal game is the one which everybody wins. Heres, it will be remembered, was a brilliant Hoh player. The idea of a *second* Plan, to accomplish what even the initial Planners had assumed to be beyond their talents, was, in Heres' eyes, *the* masterstroke.

Eleven thousand years of history demanded of the people of Euchronia a commitment—a commitment that was clear, altruistic, and ambitious. The declaration of the Millennium had left not only the Movement but the entire civilization stranded on a spiritual desert island. The age of psychosis could never return, and the i-minus effect seemed to assure social adjustment, and therefore social sanity, but Euchronian culture was nevertheless dangerously full of alarm signals. Rypeck had read those signals, and Rypeck had been on the borders of fear and anxiety for years. Heres had read the signals, too, but Heres had a cool head. Heres had faith. And he had found the answer—the political and intellectual *coup de grâce*. Barring all accidents, not only was his political future as Hegemon secured, but also the future of the Movement and the human race.

Barring all accidents.

What accidents? For one thing, of course, he had jumped the gun. There was, as yet, no report from Harkanter and his party regarding conditions in the Underworld. Politically, the right moment had come before he had all the facts at his command, and thus there was a risk—of some kind. But Heres knew what Rypeck had found out about the Underworld—that it lived, that it was lighted, and that the Overworld was geared to resist the invasion of its life-forms. He also knew what Abram Ravelvent had discovered—that materials were constantly exported from the world above to the world below—materials like steel implements and books, which spoke conclusively of human life and some degree of human culture. Heres knew little enough about the Underworld, but it was enough to be *sure*. It mattered little how severe the conditions in the Underworld might be, or how savage the people. The *magnitude* of the task was, thanks to the Planners' precedent, quite irrelevant. Heres was quite confident that any accidents of circumstance could be overcome. He still had faith in himself. Rather more than that, in fact—he had ultimate faith in the essential nature of things, in the fact that the situation (*all* situations) not only provided an answer by which everybody could win, but were so structured as to *demand* such an answer. This faith did not arise from the fact that he was a devoted Hoh player—the reverse was actually the case. That was the way Heres conceived of the universe working. It was his understanding of existence. Hoh was only a model—a simulation—of reality.

Heres also knew that he had sidestepped the thorny questions which the Magner affair had initially asked. Those questions, framed by Enzo Ulicon, had seriously disturbed Rypeck (who was, of course, ripe for disturbance). In Heres' scheme, there were no answers to those questions. Instead, Heres was prepared to hope that he had rendered the questions irrelevant and immaterial.

Magner had had bad dreams. Terrible dreams. That meant that either the i-minus effect was *not* effective, in his case, or there was another input into his dreams—presumably tele-pathic. Ulicon had held the latter alternative to be the more likely. Heres had said nothing, but he had always preferred the former. He had already known—as everyone with eyes to see must have known—that the i-minus effect was not operating as per prescription in the Millennial society. No one knew how, or why, it was going wrong, but it was. Heres was inclined to attribute the deficit not to the i-minus agent but to the social psychology of the people. I-minus favored social adaptation, the establishment of social values as absolutes. If i-minus was failing, then it was for lack of social values rather than lack of adaptive capacity, so Heres thought. Given a plan—an ideal, a great social goal—then i-minus would work again. So Heres believed. He had seen Magner as the tip of an iceberg rather than a unique case of something new.

Heres was prepared to assume that the second Euchronian Plan would solve everything. His understanding of reality encouraged him to make this assumption. He was aware, however, that it remained an assumption. He was not blind to the possibility that some unforeseen, incalculable factor might yet be thrown into the equation. He was mentally ready for such a thing to happen. It did.

6.

Jervis Burstone, whose amusement in life was to play God rather than to play Hoh, was in the Underworld, waiting. Usual-ly, Ermold was at the rendezvous before him, unable to control his eagerness to get hold of the gifts which Burstone brought and dispensed so magnificently. (They were not quite gifts, but neither Ermold nor Burstone knew why the pretense of trading was maintained. They both believed that what Burstone took in return for his goods was worthless.)

Burstone sighed. He knew that Ermold was not going to come. Late meant never, in the Underworld. It was a world which did not offer second chances to its people.

Ermold had been a good contact. He had been the nastiest, most vile of all the men that Burstone had had to deal with, and by virtue of that fact he had looked to have a good many years in him. But time seemed to move so quickly here. A man might pass from maturity to senility in a matter of weeks. The people of the Underworld seemed to live their lives inside a span of time which Burstone hardly noticed in passing. Burstone could remember the contact before Ermold as if it were yesterday. And the one before that. He would remember Ermold with crystal clarity when three more contacts had all fulfilled their purpose and rotted into the stinking, polluted dust from which they came. That was the way of things.

Burstone waited, unwillingly, glancing at his wristwatch every few moments, giving Ermold the time that was his due, but begrudging the filthy savage every second of it. Burstone did not like the stillness and the alienness and—more than anything—the cold, steady perpetual starlight. He sweated, and knew that he was slowly absorbing the stink and the foul taint of the Underworld. Once back on top he would have to slink home like a rat in the shadows, to bathe for an hour and plaster himself with the medicines which would save his skin from rotting away, and save his body from the vile diseases he inhaled with every breath. If only he could wear a mask—a proper mask rather than a wad of cotton wool and a piece of perforated plastic. But he had been warned against masks.

He was afraid, as well.

But the thrill of fear, and the rather less conscious thrill of pollution were almost life's blood to him. He needed them. They gave something to him which he could not hope to find in any other way. The tainting of his body and the washing clean, the scouring of his body with the hormonal cocktail that was fear—these meant something to him. They were real to him in a way that the diversions of the Over-world were not. The ritual descent into Hell, followed by the ascent into Heaven—this was the purpose of life. It was the focal point of his existence. It was the reason that he was *needed* by the worlds. It was his duty, his honor, and his...joy?

Burstone was a completely sane man. His dreams never troubled him.

While he waited, he drifted on an ocean of feeling. An emotional castaway.

The creatures of the underworld would not come close. The smell of him, in their senses, was just as alien to them as theirs was to him. His sharp, chemical cleanliness was an affront to them. No predator would dare to come close, and the small creatures engaged in the business of survival detoured in order to pass him by. He saw the great ghost moths fluttering between the squabs some yards away, and heard their high-pitched screaming at the very limits of his audible range, but there was not enough light for him to see anything else. He was virtually blind down here. He had a horror of darkness, too. On this, too, his soul fed.

When the time was up, he simply picked up the suitcase and began the walk back to the cage with which he could hoist himself back to the platform. He walked with an easy, measured stride, unhurried. It took courage—genuine, completely pure courage. It took strength of mind and of character. He never looked around. The thought of finding a new point of entry, of setting up a new contact, and the inevitable risks that would be involved in so doing, did not disturb him. He accepted that part of his role.

Up on top, clean and healthy, he would still feel good, even though he had not fulfilled his mission on this occasion. He would feel the satisfaction of knowing that his part was played.

He was only an ordinary man.

7.

The Hell beneath Euchronia's Millennium had not been cut from the cloth of existence in a single piece, or in a single moment. It grew as a patchwork, very slowly. The several evolutions which took place beneath the slowly expanding sections of the Overworld platform had every chance to discover new ways of coping with the conditions of life. The adaptation of surface life to Tartarean circumstances took place according to several different patterns. Each pattern was a collaboration between chance and choice. When the platform was complete and the Underworld was sealed—several thousand years after the process was begun—the patterns came together, and a new collaboration begun. (Collaboration in the Underworld did not take the same form as collaboration among the Euchronians. It took more familiar forms, like war—the war of nature: natural selection.)

There was no section of the Underworld under which the ecosystem of the old world failed to adapt to new circumstances. The adaptation was costly—the mortality of species was over ninety percent, and the mortality of individuals within species that survived was often on the same sort of scale. Some surviving species, on the other hand, proliferated vastly and enjoyed altogether unprecedented success. All the surviving species were unstable, and remained so. By the time of the Euchronian Millennium, some kind of stability was just beginning to assert itself within many communities of organisms, but on the previous evolutionary scale several eons of progress toward balance had been lost. Curiously, almost half the loss had taken place *before* the Plan got under way.

Homo sapiens was the species which adapted most easily to the new regime, and by his active interference he encouraged and assisted many other species to do likewise. (He also discouraged and prevented one or two, but his positive success was much greater than the negative corollary.) The Euchronians had very unkind things to say about the men who stayed on the ground, but it was not the fact that they resented the work and the dedication involved in commitment that made most of them do so. In point of fact, the weak and the degenerate almost invariably joined the Euchronians, fearing the darkness and the wild world more than they hated the work and the regimentation. The Euchronians at least provided food and shelter for their people. On the surface, there were no guarantees. The people who stayed on the ground at the end—who actually went into the Underworld rather than join the Plan (as distinct from those who simply retreated from the encroaching platform)—did so because they preferred their own idea of freedom to that of the Euchronians. They wanted freedom *from* the Plan, and they were prepared to accept Hell instead of the promise of Heaven for their children's children, in defense of that idea of freedom.

There was, of course, a great deal of fighting between the Euchronians and the men on the ground while the platform was growing. The supplies which kept the Plan going came from the ground—from the land of the men who could still make the land provide. In return, that land was eaten up as was the derelict land. When the landowners would not supply the Euchronians, the Euchronians took what they needed. When they cooperated, the only gratitude they received was the offer to join the Plan when their land, in its turn, came to be covered over. The Euchronians won every fight. They had the numbers and they had the organization. There was no way the men on the ground could defend their world. They had to take one of the new environments which was offered to them—the proto-Heaven or the neo-Hell. From the Euchronian point of view, that was no choice at all. Not everyone saw it the Euchronian way.

Hell was not kind to the men who chose it. The old world had been past redemption in terms of the human civilization which had grown up in it. From the point of view of society in the second dark age the world was ended, doom had come. But a derelict world is not a dead world. Life continues, somehow. Always. The old order was finished, and chaos was come, but life went on. Even the imprisonment of the old world—its condemnation to perpetual darkness—could not make life extinct within it. The old species had to die by the thousand, and those which survived did so at tremendous cost, but the cost of evolution in terms of necessary death is always less than the cost of not evolving. The genetic heritage of the survivor species was ruthlessly stripped and rebuilt, with selection operating at very high levels and evolution being forced at a tremendous rate, but they could take it. Just. Adapt, or perish, was the only law. It applied to *Homo sapiens* no less than to all the other species. The cost of human survival was a complete genetic overhaul of the species. The men who went to Hell wanted freedom. Freedom from Euchronia they won, but freedom from evolution they could not have.

Evolution in the Underworld was necessarily rapid. A characteristic tachytelic pattern developed: divergent evolution of forms, rapid speciation, a high rate of extinction and specific genesis. An evolutionary explosion. It had happened before, on the Earth before man, but the evolutionary change of gear which took place when the Underworld came into existence saw the greatest-ever increase in the rate of evolution—the biggest explosion of them all. It echoed through the ages which followed, and would echo for many more. The impact was only just *beginning* to die when the Euchronians, in the Heaven which they had built up above, completed their Plan.

Man—omnivorous, intelligent, at the very highest level of the biotic hierarchy—changed least of all the species in the Underworld. Even man became not one species, but several.

The greatest evolutionary boost was evident in the semi-sentient species which had cohabited with man in the concrete jungles of the age of psychosis. They had the capacity to adapt *if* they could make the leap to full sentience and change their physical form in order to cope with a complete reorientation of their survival strategies. Some of them made that leap. Some became extinct because their gene pools drained dry in the attempt.

At the lowest strata there was complete reorganization. Millions of years of plant evolution went to waste, and progress began again with the lowest forms—the algae and the fungi. The stratum of the primary consumers in the animal kingdom was likewise completely refurbished, but here there were already patterns of life and forms of being which were useful. The crabs of Tartarus were not the crabs of pre-historic ages, nor the moths, nor the cockroaches, nor even the multitudinous worms, but the names did as well for the new versions. There are only so many ways to design an animal, and most of the models had been ready in the prehistoric world.

The microbiotica, of course, were reorganized on the same scale as the plants and lower animals, but from the macrobiotic point of view the revision was quite invisible. There are even fewer ways to design a bacterium or a protozoan than there are to design an animal. Form and function survived despite the fact that genetic complements had to be given a complete overhaul. The bacteria had the least difficulty adapting. Bacteria always exist in extreme circumstances.

From the microbiotic point of view, the division of the world into Heaven and Hell was virtually immaterial. A trivial incident on the path of existence. As if an immortal were stung by a bee....

8.

Camlak did not hurry along the road to Lehr. He walked steadily, at a pace which he could sustain for many miles. He was forced to import a rather mechanical quality into both his thoughts and his actions. It was necessary to the situation. He already knew, in his heart, what he was going to see when he finally looked out over Dossal Bog, but he advanced toward that moment nevertheless. He would have to meet it.

Once he was past the hill called Stiver he left the road proper, and bore slightly southwest, taking higher ground so that he could command a good view of what was ahead of him. He did not climb to the ridges but merely moved as a hunter might, close to the road but not too close, stalking its length, tracking its curves. The stars were less dense in the roof of the world over these dried-up, coarse lands, and the light they shed was not bright, but Camlak had good eyes, and there was light enough for him to see what he needed to see.

And eventually, his assumed mechanism brought him to the climactic vision. From the slopes of the hill called Solum he could see the road as it straightened out to cross Dossal Bog. He could almost see the shadowed walls of Lehr itself in the furthest distance—or he thought he could. Perhaps it was just a suggestion of shadows—an imaginary goal to draw travelers on ever faster, until they dropped from weariness with the vision no nearer.

The women fleeing from Shairn had gone a good way down the road. They were nearly a mile away from where he stood.

The Ahrima had come down on their backs. The bundles they had carried were scattered in a ragged line for a quarter mile behind the place where they had been caught. The crowd had scattered both ways into the bog. Only a handful had died on the road. Camlak knew that the women and the children would have run into a radioactive waste, into a living fire, rather than stand and wait for the Ahrima. And the marauders would have followed them to cut them down. And come back again to join the horde.

Camlak wished the bog was one vast quicksand, to have sucked the Ahrima down after their prey. But it was not. It was only a bog. The corpses were sprawled across the dark tussocks, half-swallowed by the mud, floating on the pools of stagnant water. The Ahrima had caught their prey, had enjoyed their massacre, and had gone on. Perhaps two or three Ahriman warriors had been trapped in the bog, or knifed by the women, but only two or three. No more. How many of the Children of the Voice had escaped? How many infants had found a hiding place? More than two or three, no doubt. Twelve. Or twenty. But how many of those would survive, in the long run? The same two or three. Maybe none. Wherever they went—forward, or back, or just on the road, there would be enemies enough for all of them.

Camlak could read the whole story written in the dim scene which extended before his eyes, illumined by starlight. It was no more and no less than he had expected. He had not expected the men of Lehr to come out and try to cover the retreat. But he had had to go on to the end of the story in any case.

As he stared out from his vantage, he felt very little emotion inside himself. He did not curse, and he certainly did not cry. He merely looked, and let the looking soak into his being. He let the sight imprint itself on his memory, becoming a part of him. That was enough. There was no need for fury or mourning. The time for those was past, left behind in Stalhelm, even before the battle and the burning.

He would follow Nita, now. And when he found her....

He knew no more. The alternatives which he would find then would have to be discovered. They were not ready in his mind. No such alternatives had ever been shown to him, except in his dreams. In his dreams, they were phantoms. He did not know what it took to clothe such phantoms with reality. He would live, but he did not know how, or why. Those answers were lost, lying amid the dead like the trampled, shattered bundles the women had carried out of Stalhelm in the vain attempt to wrap up their lives and steal them away from the Ahrima.

He could see the Ahrima. He could see their fires, at least. Whether the fires were at the walls of Lehr, or still some miles away, he could not tell. Perhaps it was Lehr, or the fields of Lehr, that was burning. The light was red and blurred, a smudge in the pit of darkness which closed off the world at the limits of his visual range.

He could imagine the Ahrima as shadows within the ruddy glow, shadow-monsters with their heads encapsulated by grotesquely huge horned masks. Men taking the form of beasts, accepting the role of the beasts, prideful of their bestiality. Black shadows in the light, clothed in smoke. The masks would shine, in the flamelight. The eyes would sparkle through the eyeholes.

The Truemen, thought Camlak, would have it that the Children of the Voice are animals. They claim that we pretend to manhood, that our selves are false. But the Truemen are masked now, their eyes glittering like the eyes of the Ahrima, fugitive within the masks, hiding from the fire and the blood. A worthless attempt to save their worthless lives. Who are the fake people?

Inside himself, Camlak asked the question of his Gray Soul. He did not expect an answer.

As he turned away, content not to know the fate of Lehr and, ultimately, of Shairn—at least for the time being—he sensed a movement on the slope above him. Someone was stalking him as he had stalked the road. They had not been behind him long, but they were there now.

Ahrima!

He carried a bow and a long knife—he had left behind the axes and the Ahriman swords, which were too big for him. He put the bow across his back and drew the knife. He moved toward the sound, extending the blade before him. A shape rose from the barbweed, coming out from the hiding of a shallow recess. Empty hands spread wide.

"No," said the shadow. "Friend, not enemy."

Camlak did not need the sight and the sound to know. The way the shape had risen had testified to its crookedness. It was Chemec, the warrior with the bent leg. Of all the warriors, Chemec had lived. Chemec and Camlak. Why?

Chemec knew. Chemec knew his bent leg, and knew that it had taught him all he needed to know about the art of survival. He had had to learn new ways to run, new ways to fight. It had to be Chemec that lived. No one else, save by luck.

Camlak sheathed his knife.

"It would be you," he said. "It had to be." There was naked bitterness in his voice.

"And you?" Chemec retaliated. "I could say the same. We are

both alive instead of dead."

It was true enough. Chemec flinched as he spoke, ready to run if Camlak remembered any one of a dozen times that Chemec had cast doubts on his manhood. Chemec had been a warrior when Camlak was yet a child. But Camlak did not remember now, and he did not react to Chemec's words. It was all over.

After a brief silence, when Camlak would not look at Chemec, and Chemec would not look at Camlak, the crippled warrior asked: "What now?"

It was a plea for guidance—a warrior asking the decision of the Old Man, whose function was to decide. Chemec had been a warrior while Camlak was a child, but Camlak had killed the harrowhound and played the Sun in the communion of souls. Even so, Camlak was faintly surprised. He could not help but feel that perhaps Chemec was mocking him.

"Stalhelm is dead," said Camlak. "Do what you like. Anything."

Chemec shook his head. "I'll come with you," he said.

"No," said Camlak.

Chemec did not understand. This would not have been Yami's way. Yami would have welcomed him. It would have been Yami and Chemec, together.

"We might go east," said Chemec. "The Ahrima will turn south."

"North," said Camlak.

"We go north?" Chemec deliberately misunderstood.

"The Ahrima," said Camlak. "They will go north, into the heartland, to rip the bowels out of Shairn."

"We go north," suggested Chemec. "To fight."

"No," said Camlak again. "You go."

Chemec was silent.

"It's dead," said Camlak. "It's finished. Stalhelm is over. A memory, nothing more."

Chemec still said nothing. He could not accept it. It was beyond him. He was getting old.

Camlak looked at the man with the twisted leg, and remembered that this had been his enemy. This man might even hate him, and hate him still. But he was ruled by the way, by the rule of the ritual.

"I don't want you," he said.

Chemec waited. He could do nothing but wait.

When Camlak turned away, Chemec followed him. When Camlak half-turned, Chemec dropped back, but still followed.

Camlak went north, but not to the heartland—not to fight. The heartland was well to the west of north, bordered by the vast Swithering Waste. It was into the Waste that Camlak went, heading for the great metal wall.

Chemec followed, with infinite patience.

9.

As Burstone turned to lock the door behind him they slipped out of the shadows, and when he turned, they were there, blocking his way and pushing close to back him up against the wall. The alley was quite dark—it existed only to hide away the door from which Burstone had come. For a moment, he thought that they might be technics, on legitimate business, wanting to go down to the distribution units and wondering what he was doing there. But that was a hopeless wish. They had been waiting. For him. They knew who he was and where he had been.

He didn't know whether he ought to be scared or not. No one had ever interfered before. He *was* scared.

One of them took the key from his hand. Gently. Then he put it back into the lock, and turned it. The door eased open when it was pushed. The dim light of the machine room filtered out, throwing vague shadows across the faces of the two men.

Burstone overcame his momentary paralysis.

"Do you want something?" he asked.

"The suitcase," said the man who held the key. He was a tall man, but that was all Burstone could be sure of. The glimmer of light wasn't enough to let him see any facial details. It was much darker here than in the Underworld. The *real* stars were so faint.

He could hear the keys being clicked back and forth in the tall man's hand.

"We just want to talk," said the other man. Burstone became conscious that he was being held by the arm. He wrenched slightly, and felt himself released. But they still stood in his way, pinning him in the corner of the blind corridor. The door oozed shut, and the darkness became total save for the pale silver sheen of the sky, high above.

"Who are you?" he asked.

"Suppose we were the police?" countered the tall man.

"Suppose you were?" said Burstone.

"That's right," said the other man. "You don't have anything to fear from the police. Nothing to hide. You're doing nothing illegal. Any man in the world is perfectly entitled to take cases full of...whatever...into the Underworld. The police wouldn't be interested. Surprised, but not interested. So who would? Who'd be insterested, Jervis? You tell us that."

The calmly threatening tone somehow eased Burstone's mind. This wasn't right. Of course it wasn't right. They had no right. They had nothing against him. He wasn't doing anything wrong. The way the man spoke restored Burstone's confidence in himself. The surprise was fading. The situation was becoming known, and therefore controllable.

"What do you want?" he asked, in a cool tone which said clearly that they weren't going to get it.

"You've been followed before," said the tall man quietly.

Burstone said nothing.

"We know about that," said the other. "He didn't come back, did he?"

"Suppose," the tall man said again, "we were the police."

"I didn't do a thing," said Burstone, once more on the defensive, once more crawling back into a shell of fear. "Nothing."

"He *didn't* come back."

"No," said Burstone.

"What did you do?" demanded the tall man.

"Nothing," repeated Burstone.

"Suppose we knew what happened to him," said the other. "We know his name. Joth Magner. Did you know who it was? You must have, of course. You could hardly miss him, could you?"

"I never heard of him," said Burstone.

"You heard of him."

Burstone pushed himself out of the corner. One man—the tall one—stepped back, to remain in front of him, barring his way. The other slipped in behind him. Burstone liked the new arrangement even less than the old. He had the ridiculous idea that at any moment the man behind might crouch, so that the tall one could push him back, make him fall over, like a small boy.

"What are you trying to say?" asked Burstone.

"Briefly," said the man behind him, speaking close to his ear, "and without all the veiled threats, that Joth Magner followed you through that door a while ago, and he didn't come back. We want to talk to you. Because we know about Joth Magner and the police don't, we think you want to talk to us. All right?"

"I didn't kill him," said Burstone.

"What's in the case?" asked the tall man, ignoring the protest. "And why?"

Burstone considered the situation. He hadn't killed Joth Magner. Not quite. But he had wound up the cage, knowing that someone had gone down, and that the someone would inevitably be trapped. He knew what the Underworld was like. He knew what would happen to him if *he* came back one day to find that the cage had gone, and that there was no way home. He knew.

The worst thing was, he hadn't an answer to his own question. He didn't know why he'd done it. He'd been scared. He knew he'd been followed and he knew he was being watched. He could have just gone away and left it, but he was too frightened even to do that. He'd wound up the cage and solved the problem by elimination. He hadn't known it was Joth Magner. He'd never seen the man who followed him. He hadn't known. It was a momentary decision—almost a crazy decision. He regretted it now as he'd regretted it for a long time. He'd almost been expecting it to catch up with him. He knew that he was responsible for Joth Magner's death. He felt it. He only wished that feeling it would tell him *why*.

"Who are you?" whispered Burstone.

"Does it matter?" asked the tall man.

"Does it have to be here?"

"No. You want to go home?"

"Yes."

"Okay," said the other man, still behind him, still mouthing into his ear. "Let's go."

Burstone moved forward. The tall man stopped him by jabbing a key gently into his chest. "I'll take the case," he said.

Burstone surrendered the case. Then they went back to the cars, and he led the way home.

10.

"Can we forget about the game, now?" asked Burstone.

"I don't know," said the tall man. "I'm not sure that it's over."

Burstone felt better in the light. Now he could see the two men they did not seem so fearful. His feeling of guilt had faded, to some extent. At the back of his mind, behind even the guilt, was the conviction that whatever happened, it was all all right.

"It's only just beginning," commented the other man. He was the younger of the two, slighter in build and sharper in the features. The older, bulkier man had a sallow complexion and gray eyes, which made him look somehow faded. Maybe careworn.

As Burstone studied them, so they studied Burstone. He was small, very dark and apparently strong. Hard and compact. He also stank, but that didn't surprise them. They knew where he'd been.

"Who are you?" the tall man asked him.

"You know who I am," said Burstone, faintly surprised.

"Who are *you*?"

"We know your name," said the man with the gray eyes, "but we don't know *you*. We don't understand you. We can't figure you. You work in secret, in back alleys and dingy passageways. You fetch and you carry back and forth from the sewers. You work hard at it, like a little brown ant. And for what? We can't even guess. Why are you invisible, Burstone? What makes you work so hard behind the scenes, carrying out your little jobs in utter silence, while the rest of us don't know what, or how, or why? That's the *you* we want to know. Not your name."

Burstone looked up at him. "I'll settle for the names," he said. "For now."

The younger man laughed briefly.

"I'm Joel Dayling," said the tall man. "This is Thorold Warnet."

Burstone knew that he knew at least one of the names, and he groped for the memory. He found nothing specific, but he discovered an association of ideas—a label.

"Eupsychians," he said. "What's it got to do with you?"

"That," said Dayling, "is what we want to find out."

"This has gone on long enough," said Warnet. "All right. You know who we are. You know what kind of a lever we hold. You can deduce why we want to know. The Underworld is suddenly a matter for concern. We need to know about it. You can tell us. We want to know what you know, and we want to know who else knows it. That's all. We just want the truth, for once."

Now that Burstone knew who he was dealing with, he quickly recovered the last vestiges of his composure. He no longer feared exposure—not by the Eupsychians. He would be protected against the likes of them. His work was important—theirs was subversive.

"I can't tell you," said Burstone.

"Why not?" demanded Dayling.

Burstone looked blank. It was a question he had not expected.

"It's nothing illegal," explained the tall man. "We accept that. If you like, we'll take your word that you had nothing to do with Joth Magner's disappearance. If you like, and provided that we have something else to occupy our minds. We accept that everything that you do is perfectly in order. You could do it in the broadest daylight on a holovision spectacular, and we wouldn't care. But you don't. You do it in secret. Why?"

"It's better that way," said Burstone.

His tone was flat, and it was obvious that he was repeating something he had been told—something that he accepted without question.

"Open the case," said Warnet. Burstone reached out for it reflexively, as if to stop them, but Dayling had it safe. The tall man fished out the keys which he had confiscated from Burstone, and began to compare each one with the lock on the case.

"*Somebody* knows why all this is happening," said Dayling reflectively, while he sorted through the leaves of metal. "It just isn't us. Maybe it isn't you, either, but maybe between us we can work it out. *Do* you know who you're working for?"

"Of course," said Burstone. Immediately afterwards, he wished that he hadn't said it.

"But are you right?" Warnet intervened. Burstone's eyes flicked back and forth from the hasp of the case, where Dayling's hands were working unhurriedly away, to the sharp, aggressive features of the young man.

"What do you mean?" asked Burstone.

"I mean," said Warnet calmly, "that you might be wrong. If this thing is so secret, maybe they tell *you* lies, too."

"Nobody tells any lies," Burstone contradicted him.

The lock on the case gave way, and Dayling laid it down on its side, then lifted the lid. Inside the lid, supported by a double row of clips, was an assortment of metal implements. Knives, compasses, zip fasteners—a completely crazy assortment. In the body of the case there were a few heavier, more complex pieces wrapped in transparent plastic film, heavily greased. Two drills, two axe-heads and the blade of a scythe. Dayling lifted these out, one by one. Beneath the worked metal was a layer of books—not flimsy printouts from a household deck, but sturdy things, printed on heavy paper, bound in black plastic. They had been put together, obviously, by some complex accessory to the usual deck facilities. The sort of thing a collector might have. The world was full of collectors, despite the fact that almost anything could be had on demand from the cybernet. Most people liked to set aside some small area of experience as "theirs" and pander to their pretensions of uniqueness. Some people still liked to use books as of old—the "real thing."

Dayling pulled out a few of the books. There were some boxes stacked among them—boxes which proved to contain sets of small things—scissors, needles, even surgical instruments. Dayling put them all carefully aside. When the case was empty he surveyed the displayed contents with a bewildered expression. He picked up one of the zip fasteners as if it was a snake, looked at it for a moment, and then dropped it with a gesture of annoyance.

"You didn't manage to deliver it, did you?" said Warnet quietly. "This is your end of the deal. You supply the Underworld with trade goods like the prehistoric Spaniards dealing with the Indians. Or is it more like the slavers, buying Africans with colored beads and mirrors? No colored beads, though. I bet you've taken down a mirror or two in your time, haven't you? Do you really think it's safe to give them all those sharp things? And what about the books? Aren't you afraid they might learn something?"

Dayling was looking at the books. "It's a peculiar selection," he said. "Not really *selected* at all. No pattern. History books, novels, elementary science. Memoirs of women of note...why on Earth...?"

"I see," said Warnet. "It's all backwards, isn't it. The books are the *real* exports. The useful stuff is the sugar on the pill. You're *trying* to educate them, aren't you. Missionary service."

"But why?" said Dayling.

"More immediately," mused Warnet, "what for? What would you have brought back with you if you *had* managed to dispose of this little load? Come on, Jervis, what do they give you in return? What's in it for you?"

"Nothing," said Burstone. "I mean—nothing in it for me. What they give me isn't mine."

"Nor is this," said Dayling. "It's ours. It belongs to the world. Production capacity of the cybernet. Loss of materials. Energy budgets. This is work, and time, and money, And it's all waste. It's all going down into the sewers. For nothing. What do we get in return?"

"Books," said Burstone, capitulating with the inevitable. "Their books. Scratches on bits of cloth and paper made of fibrous fungus. Hardly anything. What they can scrape together. Sometimes *their* trade goods. Colored beads, ornaments, carvings."

"No mirrors?" said Warnet.

"No."

"What's it for?" said Dayling. "Collectors? Scientific studies? Art lovers?"

There was silence. It was slow and uneasy. Finally, Burstone broke it. He revealed what he had been holding back, not even knowing why he wouldn't say it.

"It's part of the Plan," he said.

For a moment, there was blank misunderstanding on the faces of the Eupsychians. They both jumped to the conclusion that he meant the Plan which Heres had proposed only hours before. That was uppermost in their minds. Then, belatedly, they realized that he meant *the* Plan. The first Plan.

"But it's finished," said Dayling.

"Some of it," said Burstone. "But there are some things that can't finish. Won't ever finish."

"Are you trying to tell us," said Warnet slowly, "that this has been going on throughout history? For thousands of years? For all the time that the Overworld has existed we've been exporting materials into the Underworld? Supporting it, sustaining it, helping it? Is that what you're saying?"

"Yes."

"And the *Council* is behind this?"

Burstone hesitated, and Warnet pounced on the hesitation.

"They don't know, do they?"

"They must," said Burstone. "Heres, at least...."

"Where does it all go?" demanded Dayling. "All the things you bring back. Where do you send them? Who keeps it all? One of the Institutes? The Museum? The Colleges?"

To all of the suggestions, Burstone shook his head.

"So who?" Dayling kept on. "Who's doing the research? Who's supplying the stuff? Who's behind it? And what do you mean by saying that it's part of the Plan? Who told you that?"

Burstone said nothing.

"We want the names," Warnet said, in a soft voice. "That's the one thing we must have. We need the names."

"There's only one," said Burstone.

They waited for him.

"Sisyr," he said.

11.

From time to time, Iorga was forced to leave the fire in order to go foraging. The fire needed to be fed, Aelite needed to be fed, and so did he. It was no easy task to live off the Waste. Whatever was edible was being consumed even as it grew, by myriad consumers who were likewise eaten while they fed. In order to eat in the Waste, one had to compete with other eaters, and also with the eaten. It was not so bad, if one could move through the bad land, because few eaters roamed far in the foul swamps. Iorga had hoped to beat the Waste, to keep moving, but that was no longer possible. Aelite was still, now, and what was still was eaten in the Waste. He could protect her while he was with her, but while he was apart....

It was difficult to feed the fire, too. Food for fires was as difficult to find as food for stomachs. With things as they were Iorga needed a bright fire and good food. For Aelite's sake. She would not recover from the smoke-cloak which was eating her slowly if all she had to eat herself were white worms and bog weed. If they had been on the move, they could have sustained themselves on a diet like that, but while they were forced to wait in the heart of the festering wilderness, they needed far greater reserves of strength and health.

So Iorga searched for special plants—sweet ascocarps and bulbed roots—and he stalked what animals he found to hunt. There were always many crabs, which he pulled to pieces and shelled, but crabmeat was thin and sour, and insufficient in itself. He made every effort to catch birds and bats, but it was not easy. Every now and again a starling would settle on a glued perch, or he would discover a hanging bat whose reactions were a fraction slowed by trance, but he had to count such captures as pure luck.

Every so often, when Aelite was fed, Iorga would build up the fire and search her fur carefully. The smoke-cloak had got holds in her legs and on her back, and because the silky hair grew particularly rich in just those places it was difficult to comb out the spores. Always there would be one or more which would escape to grow mycelia under the skin, and ultimately send up fruiting bodies like tiny orange star-bulbs unless they were located and burned out. Iorga had to sort through Aelite's fur patiently, guided by her itches when she was conscious and could make sense out of her own feeling. It was easy enough to pinch off the fruiting bodies but that was useless, if the infective mycelia remained. It was not enough to prevent spore formation. The mycelia simply grew, if they were not allowed to fruit. They turned the skin gray, burst and blistered the surface, caused bad pain. So they had to be burned out. But that, too, burst and blistered the surface, and caused pain, and weakened the body. It was a hard fight.

Aelite had been courageous, in the beginning. She lay quite still while he sorted out the infected spots and fired them, and she only sighed when the pain became intolerable. But lately, she was past sighing, and the stillness of her body did not reflect courage, but lassitude and imminent defeat.

Iorga knew that he was trying to fight the disease under impossible conditions, and that he was virtually certain to Jose, but he would not give up. It was not in his nature. He would not let the infection alone to claim her.

She could not be moved. The decaying mycelia under the skin, even burned out, became toxic, and the toxin would only stay in the epidermal tissues while she did not try to walk. The skin excreted the poison in time, given a chance, but it would spread if she became active.

The center of the infection was an old mycelium on her upper thigh which had been fired twice and yet still, somehow, managed to survive. Iorga dared not burn the flesh any more at that place, or the leg would die from the burning, and so he had to be content to shave off the fruiting bodies until the first burns had healed. He continually plastered the exposed skin with the pap of a red squab which he believed to be useful in healing the flesh and limiting the parasite. It may have been effective, to a degree, but without time on his side there was little enough reason to hope that it would be effective enough.

Iorga, of course, picked up the spores of the smoke-cloak himself whenever a fruiting body got the chance to distribute spores, but he had managed to prevent the infection getting a hold on his own body. It would not, provided that he was careful, scrupulous, and sensitive to the slightest risk, but he knew full well that he was running a risk.

He did not trouble to debate with himself the chances which would dictate whether Aelite lived or died. He did not think of the fight in terms of whether things got better or worse. He knew both hope and fear, but he would not let them occupy his mind or dictate to his body. He had switched himself out of the agonizing cycle of self-examination and repair. In order to cope with the situation he had deliberately relinquished what others might have called his "human" qualities. He needed to see the battle to the end, and he could not fight himself as well as the parasite.

Camlak found him while he was combing Aelite's fur. He did

not look up to greet the newcomer, and Camlak did not interrupt him, but simply sat down beside the fire to wait and watch.

When it was time, and the combing was done, the hellkin looked at his visitor closely. Camlak stared back, examining the large green eyes which glowed luminous in the firelight, with the vertical slits half-closed.

Camlak displayed his empty hands. It was hardly necessary, but it was proper. Iorga matched the gesture, sealing the truce.

"I have food," said the Shairan. "You will share."

Iorga nodded, almost imperceptibly. Camlak took what he had from his pack and began to sort it out. Until they had eaten, he would not say more. The hellkin was involved in something of his own, something difficult. Camlak did not really want to invade his privacy at all, but he wanted to help. The hellkin would not be grateful, but he would hardly refuse.

Afterwards, Camlak asked: "Have others passed this way?"

Iorga was silent, but Camlak knew that the lack of an answer was honest.

"How far is the iron wall?" asked Camlak.

The hellkin shook his head, again very slightly.

Chemec came out of the shallow water behind Camlak, carrying a handful of dead things. Small things, but warm. No crabs. The cripple looked at Camlak, and then at the hellkin. He gave the fresh food to the Old Man, and displayed empty but bloodstained palms to Iorga before moving closer.

"Smoke-cloak?" he asked.

"Yes," said Iorga. Chemec drew back. "Not here," said Camlak to the bent-leg. "We'll move on." Chemec was obviously relieved. He had a healthy fear of disease. His relief was quickly contaminated with disgust when Camlak gave the small creatures which he had labored hard to catch and kill to the hellkin. Iorga seemed hardly to notice.

When the Children of the Voice passed on into the wilderness, Iorga followed them with his eyes. When Camlak looked back and saluted, he nodded in acknowledgment. When they had gone, he went back to staring into the fire. Not until they were well away did he begin to rip up the fresh meat with his teeth, tearing away the fur and ripping the meat from the tiny, thin bones before he pressed the pieces into Aelite's mouth and helped her to swallow.

12.

"Why did you do that?" demanded Chemec.

"He needed it," said Camlak.

"So did we."

"Then we catch more."

"You're a fool."

Yami would have threatened to kill him if he'd said that. In fact, Chemec couldn't think of any man who would accept such an insult. But Camlak didn't touch his knife.

"If you follow me," he said, "you accept my way. Go back. Go into Shairn. You can live whatever way you want there."

Chemec asked himself why he hadn't gone into the northlands of Shairn, instead of following Camlak into the Waste. He could find no reasons, or none in words. The reasons existed, but Chemec simply could not articulate them. While he could not articulate them, he could not cope with them. They compelled him. The force was the power of collective identity—when Camlak had played the Sun to Yami's Star King he had taken into himself the greater self that was Stalhelm. Chemec was still linked to that greater self. Helplessly.

Camlak had the words to reason with, but he was not sure of himself. In his mind, he had buried Stalhelm. He did not want Chemec. But he knew that the only way to get rid of the cripple would be to kill him. That, he would not do. He genuinely did not wish to kill—not Chemec, not anyone. He knew that there were other ways and they were the ways that he wanted to find. He was certain that with the aid of his Gray Soul he could find them. In the meantime, he would put up with Chemec, if not Chemec's ways. They were bound together by a tie of some kind.

"Where do we go after the wall?" Chemec wanted to know. "If we find Nita, what then?"

"I don't know," said Camlak. "Across the darklands by the road of stars. North and further north into nowhere. Maybe to Heaven. Anywhere at all."

Chemec set his teeth tight about his tongue. The ideas themselves were enough to frighten him.

13.

Elsewhere, Joth Magner was also having trouble with parasites. On his back, out of sight beneath his shirt, he had allowed a handful of bulbous growths to develop. The spores had probably slipped down the back of his neck and stuck in his sweat. He had taken no notice because they gave him no pain, even when they grew into him. Had Nita or Huldi been able to see them on his skin they would have known enough to cut out the growths at the earliest possible moment. When Joth finally paid some attention to them and asked questions, the parasitism was well under way. Nita told him that something had to be done, and that it would be far from pleasant.

"What are they?" Joth asked. He could not, even by craning his neck, see the growths, but he could feel them if he reached over his shoulder. They were hard and granular, hemispherical, about the size of the ball of his thumb.

"They have to come out," said the girl, who had no ready name for them, but who knew the kind of threat which they posed.

"I can hardly feel them," said Joth. "I'll surely not die of them." But he already knew enough of the Underworld not to take that for granted. Life in the Underworld required ceaseless vigilance in self-defense, and the taking of no chances.

"They have to come out," repeated Nita.

The daughter of Camlak knew that it would have to be

done with a heated knife, and she also knew that she had not the strength to hold Joth down, with or without Huldi's help. She found some small globular fungi with flame-red caps and offered them to Joth.

"You told me not to eat them," he said. "Poison."

"That's right," said the girl.

"Die," said Huldi. "For a while. Better that way."

"They'll put me to sleep?"

"Sick sleep," Nita told him. "But you wake, in time."

Joth wanted to postpone the moment, but in the Underworld there were no schedules in time. What was done was done. There was no tomorrow.

He put one into his mouth, and it burned his tongue as he held it there, temporarily unable to swallow. In trying to get it down he squashed it, and the bitter fire washed all around his mouth. He gagged, and almost threw up, but he managed to get the fungal cap down. Tears streamed from his eyes. Nita gave him another, and another, waiting patiently each time for him to do battle with it. When he had swallowed four, his whole head felt like a volcano. It was as if his throat was cut. Instead of lapsing into a deep and peaceful sleep the fire reached out to clothe his mind completely, sucking it into a hot, flaming prison. Only a few moments passed, however, before the pain became only an illusion, and his burning eyes refused to see. His mind melted, and caved in. He did not black out, but ascended as though upon a curtain of flame into a sky like shattered glass.

Memory did not quite desert him, although he would gladly have abandoned it wholly. He was parted from the external world, and felt absolutely nothing of the work which Nita did with the knife, but he was still alive in a world of his own—a hideous phantasmagoria of images and distorted emotions. Not sleep, but sickness—sickness of the internal self.

Outside, Nita cut out the discoid growths, and then began to trace the extent of the adventitious subcutaneous haustoria that were digging their way slowly into the connective tissue outside the scapula. Capillary blood vessels had been destroyed and the nervous tissue had begun to decay, but the great muscle was relatively unharmed.

Huldi fetched a handful of maggots from a rotting gourd, and placed them on the wound. They would eat the dead tissue, including the haustoria, but would not touch the healthy, living cells which were no use to them. When they finished, there would be a vast wound, but the damage the parasite had done in closing the blood vessels would actually help in keeping the leakage of blood under control. The difficulty would be in protecting the wound from the rigors of the Underworld while it healed.

Inside, Joth was lost in a maze of sensation which whirled him round, taunting and tormenting him with touch and sound and color. At first the crazy whirl was simply hurtful, assaulting his mind like poison, tearing at his sense of order and organization, clutching at the fibers of his being. There came a time, however, when it almost began to make sense. He found stars in the sky of his skull, Underworld stars that were still and staring, no matter whether he soared on imagined winds or huddled into a blob of jelly in the mud that carpeted the foul earth. Perpetual stars. There were creatures swarming in his inner being like the maggots that wriggled in his absent flesh; monstrous creatures which wore beast-faces or beast-masks. They all seemed preternaturally vast, and were made grotesque by virtue of the fact that all the wrong features were accentuated. What should have been negligible became prominent, and what ought to have been obvious became hard to focus on, hard even to see as the entity which it ought to have been. All the colors were wrong, unbalanced and un-integrated. The creatures had names but the names were garbled, real but pronounced so strangely that the sounds were tangled and wrenched beyond all meaning—or all recognition of meaning

The experience was real.

It was *not* a dream.

Joth knew that. He knew that he knew it. When he woke, he would know it still. It was real. He knew because he had touched the reality of which it was a part. His body had entered into it, though his mind never had, never could. But he had seen enough, sensed enough, deduced enough to begin to understand. The dead, fetid air which groped into his lungs, the filthy water which leaped down his throat into his gullet, the steady stream of terror which ran in his veins—these things were still alien to him, but he had looked into the face of the unknown, and he had felt their touch before.

He knew.

When he woke, the first thing that he said was: "How long?"

Nita was asleep. Huldi did not answer, because it was a meaningless question and because he was not recovered enough to hear.

The second thing he said was: "Listen."

She listened. She could not promise to understand, or to remember, but she listened, as she watched. She was keeping vigil over Joth. He was dependent upon her, and she was responsive to his need. She did not know why, nor even how to ask.

She listened.

"The dreams," he said. "No dreams." He had difficulty forming the words, but he felt compelled to speak, to make real and permanent what he knew, in case it faded with the vision of hell which had come to him through the fire-mind fungus.

"Images," he said. "Through other eyes. Visions. From someone else. Sent into my mind. *His* mind. He didn't know. Something...made him receptive. He saw...with the eyes of the Children of the Voice. He dreamed their lives.... He saw with their eyes.... He couldn't understand.... He never saw.

"He didn't know."

Huldi rested her hand on the back of his neck. He lay face downwards. His head slewed sideways, his jaw resting on the ground. He had difficulty moving his mouth to form the words.

What he was trying to say was that at last he had been able to share his father's dream—the dream which had led Carl Magner to his death. He knew it, though, for what it was. Not a dream, but a jumble of sense-impressions. Leakage from a million minds.

His attempt to communicate with Huldi faded away as the sickness left him, ebbing from his mind and allowing him to fall into real and natural sleep.

He dreamed. Normally.

14.

"I presume that you have no intention whatsoever of trying to find out what went wrong with Magner's mind?" Rypeck asked of Heres.

"It's no longer important," said the Hegemon. "Magner is presumably dead, the body has not yet been recovered. If and when it is the risk of contamination may be too great to warrant doing anything with it but burning it, and even the most thorough autopsy might reveal absolutely nothing. As an individual case, it isn't worth making a big issue out of."

"You seem to have made a big enough issue out of his wretched book without very much encouragement."

"I thought you would have approved," lied Heres. "You complained about our ignorance of the Underworld. You brought to light the fact that measures were apparently taken by the Planners to secure the existence of human life in the Underworld even after the Overworld was sealed. You complain about the tentative nature of the contemporary Council's government and its lack of ideas. The second Plan is the answer to all your criticisms."

"I don't want to reclaim the Underworld," said Rypeck. "If you want to know, I'd rather see it dead. I don't believe that you want to reclaim the Underworld either. I don't think that your interest in and involvement with this crazy second Plan is serious. I think it's a political move, and twice as dangerous to us because it's not sincere.

"I can see the sense in a second Plan. You may be right in saying that it's exactly what we need. We need to rebuild the

Movement to replace some real and literal movement. But not into the Underworld. Why couldn't you look outwards, to the planets and the stars?"

Rypeck knew why. First, because Magner and his book had given Heres a convenient launching pad for the second Plan. It had allowed him to get the timing right. Secondly, the alternative plan—the outward-looking plan—was a Eupsychian catchphrase. The conquest of space. The Eupsychians had laid claim to that idea and used it as if they alone had a right to it. Heres had let them take it. Heres had no use for space travel—he associated it with the age of psychosis. Heres' brand of Euchronianism recognized one Earth and one alone, the most precious of all things.

"We have been reminded of the Underworld," said Heres. "We have rediscovered it. We can't forget it again—not overnight. We mustn't forget it again. It *ought* to be the next thing on the list of our priorities. How can we lay claim to a new world with the ruins of the old one still beneath our feet. The Underworld may be a sewer but we owe it to ourselves—never mind the people who live down there—to make it a clean sewer, hygienic."

"Do you honestly see this as a real solution? To *our* problems?"

"Yes."

"I think you're lying," said Rypeck. "Or blind."

"You've no right to say that to me," Heres told him. "You're letting your bitterness run clean away with you. You're an old man, Eliot. If you continue this way you're going to make yourself look like a senile fool. Not only to me, but to the Council—to the whole Movement."

"I'm sorry, Rafael," said Rypeck. He was genuinely sorry. His head *had* run away with him. But he was seriously troubled by the course of events. He was sure that there was something in the pattern which was more serious than Heres had ever considered.

"Can't we hold back?" Rypeck continued. "Can't we wait for

a while, until we have a chance to look at the situation from all sides? Do we have to commit ourselves now?"

"We're already committed," said Heres, positively.

"Rafael," said Rypeck, "I'm going to keep on looking for the truth in this matter. If I find that the i-minus effect is going wrong, I'll break the secret. I'll have to. Maybe you can survive that, now, and maybe I can't. I don't know. But I can't let it go on."

"If you broke the secret tomorrow," said Heres, with a confidence which he did not quite feel, "it wouldn't matter. I can justify it, now. You can't hurt me, Eliot."

Rypeck was tempted to say: "I can try." Instead, he made what seemed to be a gesture of defeat. He allowed Heres to end the interview. But in Rypeck's eyes, he could never really be defeated, because—unlike Heres—he was really not fighting for his own ends. Like Heres, he was trying to play the game the ideal way—with everybody winning—but while Heres wanted to be the architect of victory, Rypeck only wanted the answer to come out right. He needed help—not to provide the answers, but to arm him with the right questions. He needed to turn to someone outside the situation, who could see into it without necessarily being a part of it. There was one person who might be able to do that—to tell him whether Heres was steering Euchronia into disaster, and if so, why.

That person was the alien, Sisyr.

15.

They tried to keep going, but it soon became clear that it was a losing battle. Joth had not the strength, and the demands which walking put upon his body detracted seriously from the slow healing processes working on his wound. In any case, they were not sure that they were going the right way, or that they were going anywhere at all.

Nita thought that they should have stayed with the wall, and gone east, rather than striking southeast into the Waste for a second time. It was quite unnecessary for them to retrace their steps—when they had come into the Waste they were in a hurry, and had accepted the need to take a direct route. There was no urgency now. In addition, there was no real reason why they should accept automatically that they were going back to Shairn. In many ways it might be a bad idea. The whole of Shairn might be in thrall to the Ahrima by now.

Huldi, on the other hand, had been all too ready to take the obvious path, and she was prepared to be obstinate in defense of the easy decision. The unknown held no attraction for Huldi— she had launched herself into it initially merely to escape from Ermold. She felt the need of a destination of some kind for the security which the idea offered. While she was going some- where she knew where she was and why. The direct way was the only way she could really be sure of. She thought in straight lines. Once she arrived in Shairn, the problem would remake itself—the security of traveling disappears upon arrival—but that was not an immediate concern. She lived each moment as it came.

They did not know what Joth thought. He did not say. When he had encountered his father at the doorway to the upper world, the whole purpose of returning had seemed to drain away. Unlike Huldi, Joth felt his identity extended in time. He lived as much in remembrance of the past and in anticipation of things to come as in the present—perhaps far more. The death of Carl Magner had taken away both his past and his future insofar as he could perceive meaning therein. Such things are not uncommon among people who live strung out in time rather than day by day. A factor in their life is erased, and the whole integrity of life simply disappears. All the threads fall loose, no longer knitted together. The bottom falls out of the world. It is a temporary effect, in most cases—it merely requires time for the threads of existence to clot, to reintegrate into a whole. In the meantime, however, the sense of purposelessness can be overwhelming, leading to almost total loss of the sense of being in the world, of being a part of the course of events.

Joth had fallen out of his role in the pattern of life as he perceived it. He was cut adrift, and he was drifting.

There is an analogy to be drawn between Joth's situation and Nita's. She, too, had lost her father, and with him her whole life. Like him, she was drifting. Huldi, though, had cut *herself* out of the cloth of her existence. She had exempted herself by an act of will. Of the three, only Huldi really felt the compulsion to refabricate a pattern, to decide on a destination, to know what she was doing and why. Only she felt the need to rediscover a purpose in life. It was largely her instigation, therefore, which had provided the motive force to take them back into the Waste toward Shairn.

It was largely her motive force, also, which knitted them together as a group. There was no thought in her head, or in Nita's, of abandoning Joth, or each other. The three of them were bound together. The binding force might as well be called love as anything else, but it was integrative love rather than directional. Like the tension in a stretched string, it pulled in both directions—action and reaction equal and opposite. The generation of the bond of love was very largely a response to Huldi's need—she brought it into being.

16.

Joth's wound had opened, and blood was leaking slowly from the surface of the damaged flesh.

"It won't heal," said Nita, trying to mop up the blood with a soft pad of matted fungus, with little success.

"Let it dry," said Huldi. She was spearing crabs which scuttled across the broad algal fronds dipping into the water. They were resting on a patch of raised ground, but though it was raised it was by no means dry. Ideally, they needed somewhere better to rest, but the swamp was completely inhospitable in this region.

"It'll never heal in the Waste," said the girl.

"Nothing but Waste for hundreds of miles," Huldi pointed out, unnecessarily. She speared another crab which came too close. As she looked out over the vast network of green strips resting on and just below the water surface, she saw that more crabs were visible, and that they all seemed to be working their way closer. They were small, blue-gray creatures with small, ineffectual pincers. They were not a common species but they seemed to be swarming in this particular area.

"Something's attracting them," said Nita.

"It's the blood," said the human girl. "Joth." As she spoke she kicked at a pair of the bolder crabs, and sent them flying through the air, to land in among the green fronds with a double splash.

"They won't bother us," said Nita, albeit slightly uneasily. "They're too small."

"But what comes after the crabs?"

Huldi had a valid point. Scavengers which converge on wounded prey are themselves a temptation to other predators, quite apart from the fact that where one carrion-eater leads, others tend to follow. The blue-gray crabs would not feed until their target was dead, but by seeking it out and pointing the way for stronger creatures they might get to eat all the sooner. Evolution favors collaboration as well as competition.

Neither Nita nor Huldi had a weapon likely to prove very effective against larger predators. Nita had a thin-bladed knife of Heaven-metal, Huldi a larger, heavier one, but made of poor iron, dull and rusted.

"We had no trouble coming the other way," said Nita, trying to use words as a shield against fear.

"We spread no smell of blood," said Huldi. "And we were much further to the west, almost on the fringes of the poisoned land. Here it is not so dead."

"Look around for stones," said Nita. "Smash the crabs and let them eat their own kind."

But the area was not the place where stones might be found. That there was solid ground here at all was due to the proliferating plant life, which had raised itself up out of the mud, binding it and making layers of humus as one generation followed another in chaotic confusion. They were on a hummock in between two dendritic monsters whose multi-hydral branches supported vast colonies of passenger-plants and whose long, spatulate leaves and creepers formed the basis for webs and mats of lacy leaf-creatures and carpets of clinging, jelly-like tissue that was almost the texture of raw protoplasm. Such a vast profusion of life-forms inevitably attracted a complex complement of insects, and no doubt sheltered numerous potentially dangerous creatures.

"We have to carry on," said Huldi.

"It's no use," Nita told her. "He's exhausted. He's barely conscious."

Joth was not even aware of the danger. He only wanted to lie down. Had he known that his life was threatened, he would have been unable to react. He would have simply waited for death to come to him.

"We can make him move," said Huldi. "Between us."

"He's too heavy." Huldi had already known that—her statement had been wishful thinking rather than a declaration of intent. Joth was not unduly large, but Huldi was shorter and lighter. Nita was less than four feet tall, and though not delicately built, could hardly support even a quarter of Joth's weight. Though she was near maturity, by the standards of her kind, she had the strength of a ten-year-old child by the standards of Joth's kind.

So they fought the crabs, as best they could, with hands and feet. It was not difficult. But in reality they were waiting, waiting to see whether crabs were all that they would have to deal with.

17.

Huldi screamed as something surfaced thirty or forty feet away. It was a reptile of some kind, with an elongated crocodilean snout and two rows of tiny needle-like teeth spilling out of its mouth. Water streamed from its warty skin, splashing from its ridged back as it shivered deliberately.

Its forelegs were longer than the hinder pair, and armed with vicious claws. As it stood erect in the shallow water it measured five feet from hip to neck, ten or twelve from its snout to the tip of the coiling tail, still invisible beneath the frothing water. With a few quick strokes of its arms it brushed away the bulk of the weed that had clung to its body.

It moved forward.

Its large, black-slitted yellow eyes were set in the sides of its head, in raised orbits—again like those of a crocodile or a frog. It did not appear to be looking at Huldi. Instead, it followed the movements of the scattering crabs. In chasing them, however, it came closer to the two humans and the rat. It stooped forward, and its long snout went perpetually back and forth as the foremost teeth snapped up the crabs and the tongue threw them back to be crunched by the jaws. It came forward, looking grotesquely like a chicken pecking for corn. It retained its upright posture, its arms waving to maintain its balance.

It flopped forward, creating a massive splash and stirring the green water-borne carpet for yards around. In the water, it came on, with a snake-like twist and then a glide like an arrow. There was no doubt now that its attention had been caught by something larger than crabs. And yet its eyes still did not seem to look directly at Huldi or Nita. It seemed to be looking all ways at once. Its jaws half-opened in a macabre smile.

Neither Huldi nor Nita felt the urge to run. Instead, they reached for their knives.

There was a momentary flurry as the long head darted sideways to snap up another crab, and the long forelimbs surfaced to rip yet again at the clinging weed. The gliding motion ceased, and once again the great beast paused to haul itself up on to the triangle of its back legs and tail. It was slow in rearing up, and this time it had to reach out with one of its claws to grip, just for a moment, a high branch of one of the dendrite colonies.

As it steadied itself, the whole of its yellow underbelly gleamed wet in the pale starlight.

Almost without thinking, Nita threw the small knife with all her strength into the center of the yellow expanse. It penetrated, but not far enough. The hide, even there, was too thick.

The crocodilean snorted, spraying thin mucous from its nostrils. It looked down, seeming suddenly unsteady again. Its jaws yawned and one claw brushed the knife from its lodgment into the water. No blood flowed.

"Throw it!" Nita howled, as Huldi moved forward with iron dagger extended, as though she intended to engage the monster hand-to-hand. The human girl stopped, and moved back, but she did not throw the weapon. She could not bring herself to release it.

Nita went to her knees beside Joth's supine form, groping for his pack in search of something—anything hard or sharp—with which she could attack the creature.

It was moving forward again, and Huldi was moving back from it, but too slowly. It would have her within the swing of its arms in a matter of seconds.

Then an arrow smashed into the reptile's belly just above the point at which the knife had gone in. The velocity of impact was akin to that of a bullet, the momentum of the shaft somewhat greater. If the crocodilean had been a man it would have been hurled backwards. As it was, it simply lost balance and teetered. Its claws waved in the air, making circles as they searched for something to grip. One found the dendrite branch again, but it was not enough. The beast fell, twisting as it did so, coiling even as it hit the water. This time there *was* blood—the water where it fell roiled, and the foam which flew up was flecked with red.

It thrashed in the water, and another arrow hissed through the air. Nita and Huldi watched it plow uselessly into the water, and Nita screamed, very faintly, having little breath to spare.

But the second arrow was unnecessary. The crocodilean wanted no more. The pain of the one sound blow was enough.

It was off through the water, horizontally, its body snaking and its four limbs thrashing back and forth in a mad, uncoordinated attempt to add to its velocity. It hesitated once, and Nita gasped again, thinking that it was about to turn and attack, but it was only the arrow catching on a submerged root. The wrench had hurt the creature, but had only made it more determined to get away.

It might survive, but the odds were probably against it. The arrowhead would remain in its flesh, though the wooden shaft would be easy enough to tear away. The wound would prove troublesome and fester. Ultimately, in its own time, the poisons in the wound would spread to the whole system. In all likelihood, the beast would end up prey for the little blue crabs. In the meantime, it would be very hurt and very dangerous, but it would not be back.

Iorga had fired from no more than twenty feet. He had come from behind the larger dendrite. He, too, had smelled blood, but he had not come to claim his share.

"Come with me." said the hellkin. "There is better ground."

Huldi, seeing the cat emerge from the cloud of mist and flies which obscured the area beyond the dendrite, had crouched with her knife, ready to fight. But when the hellkin spoke she relaxed immediately.

Iorga came forward, shouldering his bow. "I'll help you with the boy," he said.

Nita, meanwhile, was recovering her knife.

18.

Randal Harkanter came back from a short walk in the wilderness with his gun slung over his shoulder and a big sweat-stained scowl behind his face-mask.

His select company had set up camp less than a hundred yards away from the door set in the metal wall, through which Carl Magner had come to his death. They had not found his body, although a request had filtered down from somewhere in the hierarchy of authority that they should locate and recover it, if possible. They had found what appeared to be an unmarked grave, but there was no one among them willing to take it upon himself to investigate by digging. No one wanted to get his hands dirty. The Overworld was a clean world, and its citizens had clean habits. With the possible exception of Harkanter, who had, over the years, cultivated an uncaring obliviousness to his remarkable propensity for copious sweating, the delegated representatives of the Euchronian spirit of scientific adventure were anxious to be as tentative as possible in their dealings with the Underworld. An inquiring mind was one thing—a filthy body was another. The Euchronian scientists tended to believe in *mens sana in*—and *only* in—*corpore sano.*

Harkanter alone had been prepared to undertake a march into the wilderness, and he had been overruled by the prudent majority. Investigation was a slow process—one did not rush headlong into it. It was not an attitude that Harkanter had much sympathy with, but he was well-known for attitudes at odds with the spirit of the Euchronian Movement.

As Harkanter unstrapped his gun there were a few faintly polite murmurs of interest with regard to his observations.

"Filth," he said, fixing his stare on the most convenient listener, who happened to be Felipe Rath. "Filthy, disease-ridden, vermin-haunted swamp. What did you expect?"

"Filthy, disease-ridden, vermin-haunted swamp," said Rath calmly. "What else?" Rath was squatting on an extensive groundsheet, surrounded by a multitude of boxes, trying to assemble equipment. His progress was slow and unhurried.

"Quite so," said Harkanter. "I always believed the Underworld to be a worldwide sewer. Now that we're here we find it to be a worldwide sewer. Very good. So what?"

"It would be rather ambitious," Rath pointed out, "to decide on the whole nature of the Underworld on the basis of what we see from here. No doubt what we see is representative, in some way, but a world is a big place. It can include a wide range of environments. Our world above, remember, has been shaped and Planned. This one hasn't. We mustn't expect anything like the same level of comparability between geographically separated regions. On the platform there are no deserts, and even the forests don't run wild. Here it's all wild. The old world *you* know about never really existed even then. The slick myth always outlives any semblance of the reality. You thought of this trip in terms of a safari. You're the big black hunter and we're the white bearers. But that won't work here—not even as a portable fantasy. You can act out your daydreams up above—the world is geared for it. But down here it's still real."

Harkanter turned away from the patiently working scientist. Rath had delivered his speech more or less absent-mindedly, with the bulk of his attention fixed on what he was doing. He was unaware of the poisonous expression on Harkanter's face, although the mask did not hide it.

"I was asked to lead this party," said Harkanter, half-turning in order to direct his comments back to Rath. "I was asked to come down here and find the people."

"We'll find them," said Rath. "We'll find them with *this*, if they're here to be found." He lifted up the assembly on which he was working. It looked like a toy, and in a sense it was—it would have been nonfunctional in the upper world except as an amusement. It was a robot bird armed with a camera. The idea was to send it out to map the region photographically. Its basic scheme of operation would be by remote control, but it carried enough electronic gear and programming capacity to allow it to fly around obstructions and avoid other flying creatures.

Harkanter retired to his tent to breathe some sterilized air and drink some water. When he came back out, some time later, Rath was still sitting in the same place, still working on the same device.

"Why don't you do that inside?" Harkanter growled.

"No room," said Rath. "Full up." His head gestured very slightly toward the cluster of hemispherical plastic tents, wherein other members of the expedition prepared their various endeavors. Rath was by no means the only one to have been forced to do his work in the open, but most of the others were working with rather more extensive apparatus.

"You could catch fever, sitting here in the open," said Harkanter, with dour relish. "You're not wearing gloves."

"I've heard of picking up diseases," said Rath, "but I don't think one does it in quite that way."

Harkanter gathered the moisture in his mouth, but remembered in time that he could not spit without lifting his mask. Privately, he looked forward to the wholly imaginary moment when Rath would be ravaged by all manner of Hell-born ailments because of exposing his bare flesh to the air, but he said nothing. There was no point—not now.

"You're taking your time with that," he commented.

"Time has to be taken," answered Rath philosophically. "If you get into the habit of saving it, you get out of the habit of spending it. It needs the time. What's worrying you?"

Rath knew perfectly well what was worrying Harkanter. Of all the people in the encampment, he was the only one with nothing to do. For the moment, he was the spare man. In time, he would come into his own—his willingness and determination to act, and his ability to make and force decisions would be needed soon. The scientists would be only too ready to collect trivial data till the sky fell, if Harkanter were not there to make them follow up their initial findings with some action.

When Harkanter didn't answer the rhetorical question, Rath continued. "Why don't you take Vicente out into the bush? He's got no intricate equipment to fiddle with. He probably wants to get busy collecting. Better take him out now, before the enthusiasm wears off."

"Nobody's stopping him," said Harkanter.

"He won't go out alone."

"I'm not his nursemaid."

Rath shrugged.

"It'll never get off the ground," said Harkanter, meaning Rath's electronic bird.

Rath felt it better to ignore him. One of the others—Gregor

Zuvara—observed that Harkanter was inconveniencing Rath, and came over to tap the tall Negro on the shoulder.

"I've been looking at the grave," he said.

"You're not going to dig him up!"

"It's not important," said Zuvara. "It might be Magner. It probably is. That's not what I wanted to point out. Never mind the identity of the corpse—what we ought to be wondering is the identity of the one who buried him."

The suggestion had the desired effect. It obviously had not occurred to Harkanter that it takes two to make a funeral.

"The grave is fresh," said Zuvara. "Whoever dug it can't be far away. Unless they've gone for good, they must know we're here. We haven't been very discreet. What do you think?"

"We'd better mount a guard," said Harkanter.

"That's your province," said the other man. "But take it easy. Don't start handing out hours of duty arbitrarily. Try to fit in with our work schedule, if you can."

Harkanter nodded. Satisfied that the big man now had something to occupy his time and his talents, Zuvara left him. Rath looked up and gave a brief nod of recognition. He only hoped that the mysterious gravediggers were themselves discreet. In a pitched battle, the Overworlders would win without much effort, and probably without loss, but it would be messy and unpleasant.

Rath preferred things neat and tidy.

19.

Later in the day—or what would have been the day had Harkanter's expedition been in the Overworld—Vicente Soron did manage to extend his hunt for specimens beyond the bounds of the encampment. Harkanter, now convinced of the need for vigilance, and his sour mood behind him, agreed to accompany him. Soron was determined to clutter himself up with an embarrassment of equipment and containers, but at Harkanter's insistence he also managed to accommodate a gun somewhere about his person. This, too, was not without its purpose in terms of collecting equipment, however, as it was a small compressed-air device which fired anesthetic needles. Soron considered it only reasonable that anything which attacked them should thereby qualify for the specimen collection.

Harkanter led the way into the Waste, with a confident stride that seemed likely to scatter all the wildlife from his path before Soron even got a glimpse of it, but in the meantime the collector was content to stick to the obvious, leaving the fugitive for more subtle methods at another time. Nor did he try to make Harkanter slow down or pause—it would be less burdensome to do the collecting on the way back, and it was always sensible to use the eyes well before beginning to use the hands.

Harkanter was a man of direct personality, and he had no prejudice against getting his clothing wet. He therefore strode forward purposefully, ignoring the lie of the land, and stepping knee-deep in swamp water as often as not. None of the water could seep through to his skin—he was well-protected. Soron was much shorter, and the water came up proportionally higher so far as he was concerned. In addition, it was not simply his skin that he had to worry about—his pockets were full and there were specimen bottles decked around his waist in a wide belt. Thus he was forced to pay rather more attention to precisely where he put his feet, and sometimes he walked around areas that Harkanter plunged straight into. Though he covered a greater distance, he was not noticeably slower and did not get particularly tired, precisely because he avoided the circumstances which would slow him down and sap his strength.

As time went by, Soron began to feel a certain impatience, considering that he had come quite far enough for his purposes. Harkanter, however, was unwilling to listen to his mild hints. It was not that the big man was particularly keen to make a meal of the walk in the wilderness, nor that he had anything in particular against Soron, but he could not quite help himself overdoing things, simply to make the little man suffer a little for his inconveniences.

When Soron's complaints became rather more insistent, however, Harkanter stopped for a rest, sitting down and resting his rifle in the cleft of a dendrite. He then showed no inclination to move for some length of time while Soron methodically sorted out whole plants and pieces of plants, marking the bottles and making notes in cryptic ultrashorthand on his sleeves.

"It's easier than notebooks," he explained, "and more convenient than voice records."

"Sure," said Harkanter. "If you run out of space you can use the back of my tunic."

Soron consented to smile, without making any remark of his own to cap the comment. He might find it convenient to take the big man at his word, but there was no need to say so.

"Can you bring down some of the animals when we get nearer to the camp?" Soron asked him. "Birds and bats? They won't be much use as specimens but I'd like to have a look at them quickly."

Harkanter hefted the rifle in one hand. "Wouldn't be much left of anything I hit with this," he said.

"What about the handgun?"

"You want me to hit birds with a pistol? In the *dark*?"

Soron smiled again. "I thought you could do it," he said. "I don't know anything about guns."

"I'll try," Harkanter promised, sounding less than confident.

"Thanks," said Soron.

Harkanter watched the little man working away, with infinite patience and complete confidence. A typical Euchronian, he thought. All method and endurance. Like a machine. All action under complete control. He did not think of his own manner and methods as at all mechanical, but in his way, he was as much a Euchronian as the scientist. Their differences showed up clearly, but what they had in common was not so obvious to either of them. It was because they had so much in common and taken for granted that they were so aware of the differences. But method and patience were the Euchronian attributes—not because of

Euchronian philosophy but because of eleven thousand years of the Euchronian Plan. What Harkanter thought of as his qualities of imagination and creativity were really only his uneasiness and dissatisfaction with the quality of his life. He did not feel at home in himself or in the world, but he embroidered the vague and incoherent feeling into a network of ideas and assumptions which made what was simply inconvenient into something very complex and enigmatic. The explanations which he invented to account for himself were involved and detailed, but not really relevant. His was a common enough problem, although it manifested itself in different ways in different people.

By the time that Soron was ready to make his way back to camp, Harkanter was also keen to get back. But Soron did not want to return at the same pace—this time he wanted to collect as he went. Thus, when Harkanter fell, as a matter of course, into his long, loping stride, he quickly outdistanced his companion, and had to stop to wait for him. Every time the scientist caught up, the same thing happened again within minutes. It did not take long for Harkanter's patience to wear thin. Instead of stopping to wait for his campanion he began to circle back on himself every time he got far enough ahead. His path therefore became a series of loops running alongside Soron's more or less straight line. The more impatient Harkanter got, the bigger the loops became and the more purposeful his stride.

Inevitably, he took one careless stride too many.

He sank waist-deep in a patch of glistening mud onto which he had walked without considering its implications. It was smooth and dead flat, flecked with algal growths but not covered. It *looked* like a semiliquid, if Harkanter had only paused to look. But he had not, and now he was in it, stuck firm. As he struggled, he sank further. It took him a few seconds to realize that he was in real trouble. He had placed altogether too much confidence in his protective clothing.

"Vicente!" he howled.

Soron was out of sight, but when he heard the cry he came running. Not too fast, however. When he saw what had happened to the big man he stopped running and became very careful indeed about the placement of his feet.

"Come on," said Harkanter. "Help me out."

"I'll help you out," said Soron, in a poor imitation of a soothing tone, "but let's make sure that you don't help me in."

He advanced with exaggerated caution.

"I'm sinking," said Harkanter. His voice was quite even, neither loud nor anxious. In fact, he felt somewhat at a loss. He just did not know how to react. He had had no practice.

Soron came as close as he dared. When he extended a toe to test the ground before him it gave slightly, and he lost confidence in it completely. Harkanter considered that he was being too conservative, but he realized fully enough that if they both got stuck there was no one else to come running.

The big man twisted his body, and reached out toward the nearest clump of vegetation, hoping to get a handhold. He could touch the soft green tissues of the fronds, but could not grip anything solid. Virtually all the plant life in the Waste was only facultatively photosynthetic, deriving most of its energy from alternative processes, and the highly specialized structural modifications associated with leaf-bearing were simply not basic to the Underworld way of life. Tough stems and branches existed, but they were by no means everywhere to hand. Soron also looked around for something long and tough, but there was nothing immediately apparent in the vicinity.

"Hold out the gun," said the scientist. "I'll try to pull you back this way."

"It's no use," said Harkanter, comparing his size with that of the little man. But he extended the barrel of the rifle nevertheless. Soron gripped the gunsight at the extremity of the barrel, and began to pull. It surprised neither man that he made very little impression.

"You're too heavy," complained Soron.

Harkanter perceived at this point that he had stopped sinking. The mudpool had a bottom. The problem was simply to make some progress toward extricating himself.

"I can't come backwards," said the big man. "Come around the other side of the patch and I'll try to come out forwards."

Soron picked his way carefully round the glistening spot of colored mud, and then began shedding some of the load which was inconveniencing his movements. He seemed— to Harkanter—to take a long time about it. Then Harkanter extended the rifle again, and began to haul his legs forward through the sticky fluid. Soron helped as much as he could by pulling. Harkanter flopped forward, scraping for a handhold to draw himself out more directly.

Slowly, they began to make progress. As Harkanter became more aware of the fact that he *was* able to move, he became more confident of the fact that he could get out, and this helped him to make more progress. The mud made tiny sucking noises, like smacking lips, but slowly it yielded its glutinous clutch.

Then Soron let go of the gun, and tumbled backwards, leaving Harkanter completely off balance and floundering. The big man cursed volubly, but as he splashed in the mud and twisted to save himself from falling horizontally, he saw what Soron had seen, behind him.

Something had emerged from a clump of high-stemmed growths a few yards away, and it stood looking at him with large pink eyes.

Harkanter fought to bring the gun to bear, but it was no use. It had flopped into the mud when Soron had released it, and the barrel was oozing the stuff. Even if the gun would fire, it was more likely to blow Harkanter's head off than kill the creature.

It came closer. Soron picked himself up off his back and stared at it, fearfully. He was startled by the *calmness* in the creature's bearing. It walked erect, like a man. It was looking at him without fear.

It was just about four feet tall. It was gray-furred. Its head was large, but somewhat bestial in formation. It was wearing clothes, and in its right hand—it had *hands*—it was carrying a long and rather wicked-looking knife.

Harkanter had his finger on the trigger of the rifle, ready to take the risk of firing if there was no other recourse. Was this one of the men of the Underworld? he wondered. It looked more like a giant rat. An obscene parody of a man.

The pink eyes shifted—together—from Harkanter to Soron. Harkanter was frozen still, Soron was groping at his belt.

The creature displayed an open palm. "I'll help...," it—or he—began, in what appeared to be slurred but perfectly comprehensible English.

Then Soron shot it. It collapsed, falling backwards. It was not dead, though the dart had taken it full in the chest at short range. Soron's weapon was designed not to kill. The creature tried once to rise from the ground, but it could not. It lapsed slowly into stillness.

Soron was shaking uncontrollably.

"Get up," hissed Harkanter. "Run. Back to the camp. I'll be all right. Get men. *Quickly.*"

Soron came unsteadily to his feet and set off, moving convulsively for the first few strides.

"Get that knife," Harkanter shouted after him.

Soron returned, hesitated, and then bent hurriedly to pluck the knife from the nerveless fingers of the felled creature.

"Which way?" he said, uncertainly.

"That way," said Harkanter, pointing. *"Run!"*

"Suppose more come?" said Soron. "There may be more."

Harkanter was shaking the gun, trying to get the mud out of the barrel. "That's what I'm afraid of," he said. "Get moving."

Soron nodded, turned, and ran. He was no longer careful of his ground. He had left most of his specimens behind. Impelled by a terror that was almost panic, he ran for the metal wall.

Harkanter looked after him, for a while, and then put the rifle butt under his armpit, waiting.

Secure in his hiding place, Chemec also watched. He knew better than to show himself. He had dealt with the Heaven-sent before. They were dangerous, but they were stupid. Smiling to himself, he remembered Yami's way...and he looked at the fallen Camlak.

20.

"It's very kind of you to see me," said Warnet.

"I don't have many visitors," said Sisyr. "I wish there were more. Your world long ago lost interest in me. And why not? You are ephemeral beings. We have little enough in common."

"You don't make your existence very noticeable," commented the Eupsychian.

"No," said the alien. "I don't like to become obvious. There is a possibility of...embarrassment. Of course, this is my world now. I make my home here. But it is not my world in the sense that it is yours. Your people built this world...they have a fierce pride in it. Pride means a great deal to ephemerals. Do you mind my referring to you in that way, though? Perhaps I am careless?"

"It doesn't bother me," said Warnet. "I'm used to it. I've no wish to live forever." He stopped, and there was a dragging pause which suggested that he expected Sisyr to make some reply to the comment. But Sisyr said nothing, waiting for Warnet to fill in his own silence. Warnet looked at the alien speculatively, and then let his eyes move around the room as if he were inspecting it closely.

"I know so very little about you," said the human. "As... ephemerals...we seem to be very forgetful of our friends—and perhaps our debts."

"Your people owe me nothing," said Sisyr.

"Life itself," said the Earthman. He paused again, with the same suggestion of waiting, but again Sisyr did not reply.

Sisyr was taller than Warnet by a foot, but he did not seem to be a giant. There were a number of humans who topped Warnet by similar margins. The alien's skin was red-brown; his eyes were pale blue, round, and had no pupils. He had no nose, but there was an area of skin enfolded on his upper lip that was slightly darker than the rest of his skin, and which occasionally fluttered slightly. The mouth had no lower lip to speak of—the lower jaw tucked up neatly behind the upper ridge. No teeth were visible. The whole face was dominated by the eyes, which, though very little larger or more protrusive than their human analogues, stood out by virtue of the striking color difference and the reduced lower jaw. Warnet wondered idly what range of radiation Sisyr could perceive with these eyes, and with what molecular delicacy his chemotactical sense operated. What senses did the alien possess which he had not? And what did *he* have that the alien did not. The same world, thought Warnet, and yet we might live in quite different worlds, hardly able to perceive one another except as shadows. What do I look like in his eyes? Would I recognize myself. What kind of concept does he have of my identity, or I of his? And yet we sit in the same room, and drink the same wine. We may read the same books and listen to the same music. Two worlds in one, neatly slotted together. But what do we each understand by what we read and hear? Have we so little in common, or so much...?

Sisyr's hands, too, were inhuman, although the rest of him, clothed as it was in a manner which concealed rather than exposed, seemed quite ordinary. Warnet considered the hands. Fingers, of a sort, but thin, looking like insect's legs compared to the short, squat, knuckleboned fingers which twined round his own glass. Webs extended between all the fingers and when the hands were at rest they were folded. The palms were pitted, and there were ridges of what looked like suckers round the pits. The thumb was opposable, and was much more sturdy than the other fingers—strangely jointed, with a hard, horny claw.

Warnet was particularly fascinated by the hands. They seemed so strange and complex. One could learn so much of a human by looking at the hands—what could one learn of an alien? For what was the hand functionally designed? Why had evolution favored such a grotesque shape? But this question could not be answered. The context in which it might be applied—if it was applicable at all—was something which Warnet knew absolutely nothing about. He did not even know the name of Sisyr's world.

The Earthman raised his glass slightly, looking at the clear red liquid within. "It doesn't come from some faraway world of another star," he said.

"Of course not," said Sisyr. "It is wine of my own world. This one."

"Other ships call here occasionally," Warnet pointed out. "Don't they bring you gifts...small memories...of an older home?"

"No," said the alien, simply.

"And your own ship? Do you never go into space? Voyages of discovery? Perhaps visits—after all, they come to you...do you never go to them?"

"You don't understand," said the alien. "The voyages in space...they take hundreds of years. The ships are not as fast as light. We have the time...time means little enough to us...but we do not take distance so lightly. Spacefaring is not a matter of pleasure...the kind of...adventure...which you might imagine has no meaning for us. I cannot explain—it is a difference of thought, of nature-with-time. I'm sorry."

"Do you know who I am and why I came to see you?" asked Warnet. His voice was even, and there was a hint of humor in it.

"Yes," said Sisyr, and paused. His tiny mouth moved slightly, as if he were simulating an Earthly smile. He might almost have been joining in the game of words.

"How much do you know?" asked the visitor.

"Enough."

"You know that I'm a heretic?"

"Yes."

"You know how I might choose to use the information I have concerning your...activities?"

Sisyr nodded. A casual, totally human gesture. Implying that he understood politics...that he knew how badly Warnet wanted to break the people's faith in the Council, in the Movement itself.

Warnet nodded too. "I thought you would. There's not a lot that escapes your attention, is there? You know a great deal about what goes on in your...*our*...world."

"Yes."

"Well then," said Warnet. "Which of us will sum up what we both know so that we can stray into fresh pastures?"

The alien gestured with his incredible hand.

"Very well," said the human. "I'm a Eupsychian. I'd like to be a councillor. The odds are against it. The interest in the Underworld which is being stirred up at the moment interests me greatly. I think there's potential here for political moves. Heres is ahead of himself—I don't know why, but I know that he is. There almost seems to be a flutter of panic running through the Hegemony, for some reason that I can't identify. That beautiful book of Carl Magner's has made them think. Why? It's a fine piece of work—a truly revolutionary work—but its face value is zero. It means nothing. Ergo, there must be something *beneath* the surface if you'll pardon the word-play. There is more than meets the eye.

"Burstone, for one thing, meets very few eyes. Magner knows nothing about him. An odd coincidence that two people with such dramatically common interests should be operating in complete ignorance of one another. Another...person...who meets very few eyes is yourself. This world owes its very existence to you, and yet you maintain an existence which is virtually invisible. There are, of course, any number of possible explanations for that. But how many of them also explain that Burstone works for you? He thinks he works for the Movement, but he doesn't. He thinks his work is part of the Plan...perhaps that *is* true. You, after all, know far more about the Plan than any of us.

"So, when the Underworld is suddenly drawn to the attention of people in high places—some low ones, too—it becomes apparent to thinking men that there is some mystery here. What is the whole content of the mystery? Who is involved? I don't know. I've no way of finding out what Heres thinks, or what really happened to Joth Magner, or what Harkanter is in the process of finding out this very moment. I don't know. But I do know *you* know. And so I come to you, in search of a solution.

"Is that a fair summary? Does that exhaust our common

ground?"

Sisyr was still "smiling." Warnet wondered whether it was a smile at all. Perhaps a deliberate mockery. For a brief moment, he felt a wave of eeriness as he realized that Sisyr might be registering fierce anger or carnal lust, and he—Warnet—could never know. All that passed between them must be words. Outside the words, one could be sure of nothing. Implication and inference might be vastly different. This was an alien being.

"Were you surprised to discover that there were men in the Underworld?" asked Sisyr.

"At first," said the human. "But when I thought about it, why not? I was surprised when I first met the rumor that the Underworld was a living, starlit world, but it wasn't nonsense, by any means. We didn't all come up from the surface in a long line, like the animals into Noah's Ark. The platform was raised from below—it didn't fall from Heaven. Of course there are lights in the Underworld. And why not leave them on, when the Overworld was sealed? If there were men still on the ground, it would be a gesture of common humanity.

"While I thought about Magner's book it occurred to me that there was almost inevitably a living world on the old surface. We left it wrecked, because it could support civilization no longer, but once we were gone from it the situation was vastly different, was it not? A ruined world, from our point of view, would not have to be a dead world, or a destroyed world. We came out of it into our new Heaven not because we desperately wanted life, but because we desperately wanted our descendants to live the kind of life the Planners thought was appropriate to humanity.

"It suddenly occurred to me while I read Magner's book how utterly absurd it was that we—the Euchronians—should have taken it so readily for granted that what we left behind was dead and gone for all time. Absurd...but how predictable! How typical of the Euchronian way of thinking. The Planners built their wonderful new world—thanks to you. They fulfilled their ambition of making their children into parasites, completely helpless apart from their custom-designed host. That was their ideal mode of life—the parasitic. Mechanical, undemanding, comfortable, assured not by human effort but by the endeavor—the ceaseless, ultimately *reliable* endeavor—of the machine. That's the Overworld: a gigantic, living machine, upon which we humans are content to be parasitic. Of course we forget the world which we left behind—the harsh and hostile *real* world. What do we care where the monster rests its belly? What do we care how the host has to work to make its living, just so long as it lives well enough for us to supply our own needs from its excesses? That's why we don't look up into the sky, either. That's why there's been a spaceship and a starman on Earth for ten thousand years, and yet no human has ever been into interstellar space, and no human has ever tried to build his own spaceship.

"I'm sorry. You asked me whether I was surprised to discover that there were men in the Underworld. No. Not at all. It would be more surprising, if you like, to discover that there are men in the Overworld."

Sisyr completely ignored the content of Warnet's carefully calculated outburst. He had nothing to say about the image of man as a parasite within the metal monster which he had brought into being.

"Knowledge," said the alien, apparently speaking with some care, for he spoke slowly, "is always adapted to need. One learns what one needs to know. Forgetfulness is a useful talent, as you must know. You live ephemeral lives. It is necessary that you should have a world which is...to some extent...forgettable. It is simply not possible for you to live in a *whole* world. Because of what you are, you are less than what you want to be."

"And what about you?" demanded Warnet.

"It is the same."

"You're not ephemeral. You're immortal."

"There are other limits," said Sisyr.

"Let's return to simpler matters," said Warnet. "I seem to be reaching no better understanding this way. May I, perhaps, be permitted to recall some of the things that Euchronia has found it...necessary...to forget?"

"I will answer your questions."

"You supply the Underworld?"

"I do. It has been going on for so long...it is almost a ritual now, with us—certainly with them."

"You also study the Underworld?"

"Not closely. My agents bring me their books, their work. It helps me to understand. But there is no direct study. I do not know everything about the Underworld—perhaps very little more than you have already guessed."

Warnet came to his big question. "Does the Council know that you are doing these things?"

"No," said the alien.

"*Is* it part of the Plan?"

"Perhaps. As you say, some of the Planning was mine. It would not be unrealistic to say that my actions were in accordance with the Plan, that they helped to ensure its completion without too much strife and bloodshed."

"You know that I intend to exploit this information in trying to bring down the Council?"

"Yes."

"Then why give it to me? You don't favor the Euchronians, obviously. Are you against them? Do you disapprove of them?"

"No."

"Then why help me? Why tell me this?"

"I have no secrets. Had the Council wanted to know...knowledge is adapted to need."

Warnet had finished his wine some time ago. Now he took the time to put the glass down, pausing for thought. He reminded himself that he could not make assumptions about the alien. The understanding which he had was inevitably an illusion of his own senses, only real in a limited context.

"This is your world, too," said Warnet. "Have you no interest in how it is run?"

"This is my world," said Sisyr, "but it is your society. No, I have no interest in your politics. They are a purely ephem-

eral concern. I do not want that to sound critical...you understand that I am not decrying your motives and your actions. But
I think you can see that what is important to you is virtually
meaningless to me. The society which you live in will change...
is changing. Perhaps you, as an individual, will play a part in
that change. That would be good...for you. But the Euchronian
Millennium will die, and whatever follows it will die. Ideas
will change, the labels will change, humanity will change...and
I will be here, as I am. I will not say that I have no interest in
change—I am most interested—but it would be pointless for me
to *involve* myself in any way with change. In a sense, I cannot.
I am immune to it. I could never be a part of it."

"That's not true," said Warnet. "You involved yourself with
the Plan. If it were not for your involvement, the Overworld
would never have been built. Even now, you are involved in the
determination of change in the Underworld."

"I'm sorry. You misunderstand. It is my use of the words.
When I speak of involvement, I speak from my own standpoint—you, of course speak from yours. I helped the Planners—
because they asked me to help. I accepted a contract to supply
the men on the ground—again, because they asked me for such
an undertaking. Men have involved me in what they do. But I do
not involve myself. Nor do I involve men in what *I* do."

"Suppose," said Warnet, "that you were asked to uninvolve
yourself with the Underworld. To stop supplying the ground
with materials. Would you do that?"

"If the men on the ground did not want any further aid."

"And the Council? Suppose *they* ordered you to stop?"

"The Council do not order me to do anything. I am not a part
of your society."

"There may come a day when the Council does not see it that
way."

"Then my actions will depend on the way that they see it
then."

Warnet looked at the alien pensively. "The Euchronians have
remembered the Underworld. They're going to remember you,

too. You know that, of course. Maybe from your point of view you don't have any part to play in our near future. But from *our* standpoint...you see what I mean?"

"I understand:"

"I wonder if you do."

The imitation of a smile played across Sisyr's face yet again. "I understand," he said, "according to my understanding."

"I can't keep your name out of it," said the Eupsychian. "I don't want to cause you any embarrassment. I don't want to involve you against your wishes. But there's no way you can stay buried here. Not now."

"I know," said the alien. "There is always change. Nothing lasts forever."

21.

Iorga declared that it was finished.

Joth, for that moment, couldn't meet the cat's eyes, but Nita and Huldi took the information as calmly as it was offered.

The hellkin had been fighting for his mate's life for a time which he knew no way to measure. He would have been prepared to continue the contest for twice as long or ten times as long. He had no real consciousness of what elapsed time meant. There was only the present in his scheme of things, and the possibilities of the present. He did not involve himself with his memory, save when it was pertinent to the moment, and he had no ambitions or intentions beyond that moment.

Just as Nita and Huldi had helped in his fight, so he had helped in theirs. Had they come earlier, they might have turned the fight for him. As it was, he had turned the fight for them, and that was all. The wound in Joth's back had not healed, but it was not so dangerous now. There was no infection—all that kept him from recovery was the fact that his capacity for bodily self-repair was not quite adequate to the conditions which prevailed in the Swithering Waste.

Now that Aelite was dead Iorga naturally transferred his purpose from the dead to the living. He had united his aims and his efforts with those of the other travelers, and now there were only their aims and purposes remaining. They remained his. Iorga was simply bound into the unitary existence of Joth, Nita and Huldi. He was absorbed into their bond of love. They were four people of four different races, and the circumstances which had conspired to combine them were unusual, but the bond was no less strong for any of that. For man and his satellite species to have survived in the Underworld at all, evolution had been necessary. Natural selection operates two ways: it favors the effective as well as eliminating the ineffective. Love is a force which is favored by natural selection because it leads to unity of purpose, collaboration, and the effective protection of offspring from the rigors of the environment. Evolution in the Underworld had favored love—a kind of love that the people of the Overworld would not have recognized, but love nevertheless. Factors which evolve for one purpose may often serve others, and perhaps the capacity for love which the people of the Underworld had inherited was not evolved to create ties of the specific kind which held Nita and Huldi and Iorga together with the man from Heaven, but such ties could and did form, and such ties could and did *work*.

Joth felt obliged to speak, when Aelite died, although he knew that the others were possessed of a fatalism which would not allow them to grieve. The same feeling which would not let him meet Iorga's eyes made him try to exercize his emotion in words.

"The smoke-cloak didn't kill her," he said. "You held that in check. You stopped it spreading."

"She was weak," said Iorga. "Too weak. All her strength was gone. We could not put it back."

"It was time," said Huldi. "Time for her to die."

The hellkin said nothing.

"Time was against her," said Joth. "But it wasn't just time. It was entropy. She just couldn't hold on to the sense of unity that held her together. Iorga wouldn't let her die, the smoke-cloak wouldn't let her live. In the end, she just evaporated. When neither side in a contest will give way, the rope they're pulling simply breaks. That's what happened."

They didn't answer. For one thing, they didn't understand. On top of that, it didn't really matter to them what had killed her. They did not have to explain how and why she had died. It was not necessary to their understanding. But they let Joth talk, because he did need to understand, in his own way. Joth, condemned to confine much of his being to remembrance, belief and introspection, had been the battlefield in a fight for life before, and he could not help but associate this moment with that one. When his face had been destroyed in the explosion, Carl Magner had fought for days, with the only weapons he had—more words—to make them repair him instead of ending his life quietly and mercifully. That battle had ended in life. This one had not—not for Aelite.

"What now?" asked Joth.

"We wait for Camlak," said Nita.

Joth tried to estimate, in his mind, how long it must have been since Iorga met Camlak. But he could not even make a guess at how much time had elapsed since Iorga had saved them from the crocodilean. There was no standard for comparison, no way to make a yardstick. It might have been days or weeks. The vital question was: where was Camlak now? Where might he have gone? If he were to return here, when would he arrive? Or when should he have arrived?

"He may wait for us, at the wall," said Joth.

"No," said Nita. She knew. She was sure.

"He might not be able to find us. In the Waste, he might cross our way again, and never know. We can't know that he will ever return here."

"We should go to Shairn," said Huldi, who obviously had no faith in Camlak's imminent arrival either.

"We are at the place where he met Iorga," said Nita. "He will come here. When he discovers that we have come back this way.

He will come to this place."

"Why?" Joth protested. But no one answered.

22.

Camlak never came.

Even so, they did not wait in vain. What would have happened if no one had come, Joth could not tell. In time, perhaps, Huldi's conviction that no one would come would have outweighed Nita's dwindling assurance that Camlak would return. But how long might that have taken? Joth did not know. There was no way for anyone to know. Events in the Underworld took as long as it took them to happen. That was all.

But their waiting came to an end when Chemec came into their camp and asked if he might share their food.

They had taken Aelite away from the resting place and abandoned her to the scavengers at a safe distance. It did not matter that they should have her. Joth had buried his father, but that was his way. He said nothing about what Iorga did with Aelite. That was *his* way. Chemec came to them just as they returned. He was tired and hungry. He was glad to find them, because they had warmth and food. It could not be said that they were equally glad to see him.

"What happened?" demanded Nita.

"We reached the wall—almost. There were Heaven-born. Many of them. Camlak tried to speak to them. Then he fell. I stayed in hiding. I saw them come to take him. They tied his arms—he was still, but I don't think he was dead. They carried him away. I followed them to the wall. They live there in houses like mushroom caps. They have metal—much metal. Big machines. They took Camlak into a house. The men who took him in came out again, one by one, but there were always others who went in. There were too many. I came away."

"You were going back to Shairn," said Nita.

"Yes."

"You left him to die."

"Yes."

"I don't think they'll kill him," Joth intervened. "If they tied him before they took him...they must have come down after my father, looking for the truth. Perhaps it's the men who shot him. I don't know. But they won't kill Camlak if they took him alive. He can tell them the truth. Everything they want to know about the Underworld. With his help, they can make the people in the world above believe in the Underworld. But...." He trailed off. But they wouldn't understand. That was his thought. There was no point in saying it. They couldn't understand either. Not even Nita, who understood perhaps more fully than Camlak. How could anyone understand?

What would happen when Camlak talked to the men from Heaven? Would they think that the substance of Carl Magner's dream was true? Would they want to do what Carl Magner had demanded of them? What would happen to Camlak?

"I've got to go back," said Joth. "I've got to go back, this time."

"For Camlak?" said Nita.

"I'll try," he said. "I'll try to return Camlak to you. With all my heart, I promise you. I'll get Camlak back if I can. Perhaps I can do that first. If I go back instead of him, I can tell them. They won't want to release him, but perhaps I can make them let him go. I *will* make them let him go. I might need help. Will you help?"

"Yes," said Nita, immediately. But Joth wasn't looking at Nita. He was looking at Iorga. If it came to a fight, Nita would be little enough use. Joth was thinking, at that moment, of rescuing Camlak first and going back to the Overworld afterwards. He needed a fighting man to help him—someone who could take care of trouble. He needed Iorga, who was as big as any man, and as strong. Even Huldi was too small.

"I'll help you," said the hellkin.

"And you?" Joth stared at Chemec, who was avoiding his eyes carefully while eating steadily. The cripple looked at Joth, and then at Nita.

"Will you show us where he is?" said Joth. "That's all. You're no match for a full-grown man—I won't ask you to go into the camp. But you have to show us where Camlak was taken."

Chemec nodded. For a fleeting instant, he smiled—a smile of pure joy. He had killed a Heaven-man, once. Bent-legged as he was, he had taken the skull of a Heaven-born.

It had been a good moment. That was in the days of Yami's way.

The image in his mind faded almost as it was recalled. The smile was born and died, in a fraction of a second.

"I'll show you," he said. "But I sleep first."

"We all sleep," said Joth, suddenly taking it upon himself to assume leadership. "Then we go get Camlak back."

He felt a strange satisfaction at the making of the decision. Underworld ways were infecting him. It was good to have a destination and a purpose. It was good to be committed, to know where—and when—he was. The *why* of the matter tended to get lost, but he was not so committed to the Underworld as not to know. He did know why. He had any number of reasons. The simplest of all was that Camlak had been good to him. Camlak was his friend. He owed it to the Old Man of Stalhelm to deliver him from his enemies, from those who would inevitably abuse him.

23.

The camp was sleeping. That included Gregor Zuvara, who was notionally on watch. The rotation of sentry duty was regarded as a nuisance by most members of the expedition, who felt that they had better—or at least more interesting—things to do with their time. Hardly anyone thought that it was necessary, anyhow. They had all seen the rat-man, who did not seem a fearsome creature at all: child-size and sleeping peacefully. Zuvara, who had been at least partly responsible for the establishment of the duty, was even more off-handed about it than most. His attempt to stay awake on the night watch had been distinctly half-hearted. (In Underworld terms, of course, they were *all* night watches. But the expedition was still keeping religiously to Overworld timing.) Zuvara was not expecting visitors.

The attitude of the Overworlders to the matter of security was mildly curious. It was not that they were not afraid—every one of them was fully conscious of being a stranger in an alien world. But their fear did not make them vigilant. They were unsure in their reaction to what they felt. The instinctive alertness which should have been associated with it was not quite gone, but their instincts were unrehearsed, blocked out of their being by the i-minus effect. Their fear was not constructive.

Joth Magner, though, had learned the meaning of fear. The i-minus agent had been leached from his body, and he had slept for very long periods after his initial introduction into Stalhelm. He had dreamed, and his mind had learned. Now he knew how to use his fear, how to accommodate and respond to it. When he came from the edge of the Swithering Waste into the camp of the Heaven-sent he moved like a man of Hell. Silently, carefully, balanced on the adrenalin thread of his emotional tension. He led the way, and Iorga followed. They went straight for the tent which Chemec had indicated to them, not even pausing to relieve the sleeping lookout of his gun.

The tent to which they came was one of the largest—a vast plastic inflatable supported on rigidified half-hoops. Its door was inset, with a press-seal and an antechamber. Offset from the antechamber were shower baths connected to giant steel cylinders containing a sterilizing agent. The heavy suits for outdoor wear were gathered in a long series in a second invagination of the inner chamber. Joth and Iorga came through easily, leaving both seals undone and the flaps caught back, in case a hasty exit became necessary. That they were exposing the men in the tent to possible contamination did not worry Joth. Indeed, he found a certain wry pleasure in the idea. He had been pitched into the Underworld without protective clothing, with no face-mask or gloves, and he had survived. If these men wanted to get to know the Underworld, then they could get to know it *his* way, and welcome.

Once inside, Joth searched the tent carefully with his eyes. There was absolutely no sign of Camlak. Neither cage nor coffin. There were four beds in the tent, but three were empty. Joth found this ominous. The man outside might belong to one of the beds, but if two men were missing there was only one place that they could logically be. They must have gone back to the Overworld. Carrying their prize.

The deduction, however, was not enough. Joth needed to be sure. The man who slept alone in the big tent was Felipe Rath. He was sleeping deeply—the kind of slumber which once had been called the sleep of the just. He had been working hard. His bird had gone out and returned three times, each time bringing back long series of film. He had transmitted the pictures back to the cybernet by wireless telephone, and signals had been coming back all day to the mapping deck which he had brought out. The deck had been producing photographs and numerical analyses and maps for several hours. Most of the paper he had been content to pile up for later reference, but he had been unable to resist the temptation to collate some of the maps and get some idea of the kind of world into which he had come. A good deal of the paper was still strewn on the floor beside the deck and around the bunk, but Joth managed to avoid stepping on it and rustling it. He put his hand to Rath's throat and squeezed hard, letting the pain and the asphyxiation wake the scientist.

Rath's eyes opened, the pupils recoiling and dilating as they adjusted to the dim light of the single lamp. When he saw Joth's face he was stricken by terror. It was not surprising. It had happened to many other people under much kinder circumstances.

"Don't make any noise," said Joth softly. "I'm going to let go of your throat. But if you shout I'll cut it." He showed the terrorized Rath Nita's small knife. Iorga kept well back, shadowed from the lamplight. It was bad enough for Rath to wake up looking into Joth's steel face, without having him see the cat as well.

Rath gasped as Joth released him, but did not cry out. His eyes moved away from the metal face, traveling down the length of Joth's crouching body. Joth knew what the other was seeing. Not a man but a savage half-beast in rotted clothing, covered with dirt, no doubt with a stink that was bordering on the overpowering. But Joth could smell Rath, too. He waited for the look of horror to die from the face of flesh, and for the realization to dawn, if it was going to.

It did.

"I know who you are," said Rath, in a coarse whisper which was just too loud for Joth's liking.

"I'm Joth Magner."

"I...."

"Yes. You know. You never saw me before, but you know."

"They think you're dead."

"I'm not."

"The grave! It was you. You dug it. It *was* your father. You met him. Here, at the doorway. He *did* know."

Joth put a hand to the other man's mouth. Rath flinched from the touch, an expression on his face which suggested that he had just tasted—or imagined—something extremely foul. His mouth closed like a trap.

"Shut up and listen," said Joth. "My father *didn't* know, but that's not for now. There'll be time. Later. Maybe much later. For now, I want to know what happened to Camlak. Did he tell you his name? No, never mind that. I don't suppose you gave him the chance. The man that you took in the wilderness. You know who I mean."

Rath looked at him as if he were mad. Then the Overworlder's pale eyes slipped past Joth for the first time, realizing that his assailant was not alone. Joth watched Rath's eyes widen again. He could not see Iorga's face, but he could see the silhouette, and he knew that it was not a human shape.

"What is this?" said Rath.

"Keep quiet. I meant what I said about your throat. Not for my sake. I have nothing against you. But if they see *him*, there's likely to be shooting. I don't want that. I want to know where you took the man you captured."

"It's not a man," said Rath, the strain making his voice taut and high. "It was a rat. You must know that."

Joth shook his head. "Never mind that. Where is he?"

"Harkanter took him."

"Up above?"

"Right."

"Good." Joth nodded, as though he was offering encouragement to a child. "Now tell me where. Exactly. The geographical location."

Rath's eyes flared. "I don't know! Harkanter...maybe his house, at least to start with...but I don't know."

"All right," said Joth, smoothly. "Don't panic. This Harkanter. His first name?"

"Randal."

"I can find him. That's fine. Now something else. Who killed my father?"

For a moment, Rath could find no words. It was completely unexpected. He didn't know what kind of a reply to give. From the midst of his confusion emerged the realization that Joth thought the expedition might be connected with the assassination.

"No," he said. "I mean...I don't know. Nobody knows. He was shot from a car. Ravelvent saw it. And your sister. But nobody knows who or why. We came down to find out—that as well as other things. He was murdered by a man in a car. None of us had anything to do with it. I swear it."

Joth nodded again, several times. He was thinking hard.

Rath's eyes were on the knife. "But you're a man," he said, in a voice that was even tinier than his whispers. "You're a man."

"I don't look it," said Joth, "do I?"

"You're with *them*."

Joth felt tempted to laugh. He had not laughed for a long

time.

"My father's son," he said. "Champion of the Underworld."

"Why didn't you come back? Why didn't you come to tell us?"

"I *have* come back. I will tell you. But not yet. There's something I have to do first."

"The rat?"

"The man. Camlak."

Rath shook his head, trying to move himself away from the point of the knife. But it followed him, hovering only an inch from his adam's apple. "Harkanter," he murmured. "Taken him back."

"What for?" Joth demanded. "To show off? How did they take him. Walking? Or drugged, caged, tied?"

"He was still drugged," said Rath feebly. "In the cage."

Joth took the knife away. Rath sagged slightly. There was a moment's frozen silence.

"I don't understand," said Rath.

"I don't suppose you do," said Joth, now seeming a little weak himself. Rath scanned the metal visage, no longer quite so frightening, and then he looked at the shoulder, where the livid wound showed through the vast hole in the shirt.

"What's *happened* to you?" said Rath.

"I've found out the truth," Joth told him. "In a rather more direct manner than the way you have planned. I know what this world is like."

"Your father...."

"...was wrong. But not the way you think. There's more to it than that."

"I don't know. Not yet."

"No," said Joth. "You can't." Abruptly, he stood. But he did not move away. He simply looked down at Rath. Rath stared back, the fear coming back again in a sudden rush.

"Where are you going?" he said.

"I want you to go back to sleep," said Joth. "What I tell you now is true, and you had better believe it. If you don't, or if you go against what I say, then you'll end up dead. I mean that. There are more...men...waiting out in the Waste. Don't bother to try and trap them. You won't. They'll be watching. Don't rouse the camp. Don't raise any kind of alarm. Not now, not when you all wake up to go about your business. Forget what's happened. Above all else, don't contact the upper world. If this man Harkanter is alerted, I'll kill you. If I don't come back, someone else will kill you. That's a promise. Do you understand?"

"Where...?"

"Do you understand?"

"Yes."

"You believe me?"

"Yes."

"No alarm?"

"No."

There was a pause. Joth was making every effort to scare the man into obeying him. He thought that he could do it. If not... then whatever would happen would happen. There was no way to make sure Rath kept his word, no way to exact retribution if he did not.

"What are you going to do?" breathed Rath.

Joth was searching the room with his eyes for the second time. He did not answer immediately. Before doing so, he picked up a rifle and a pistol from the table where they were ready to be picked up by anyone who wanted to go out into the Waste.

"I'm going up," he said, finally. "To the Face of Heaven."

As they left the tent, Joth sealed the flaps. But the smell lingered behind him, and Rath suddenly felt utterly contaminated.

24.

At the great metal door, he stopped.

"You must go back," he said to Iorga.

"I will come," said the cat.

"You don't know what it's like. You can have no idea. It's my world, not yours. I think I should go up alone."

"I will come with you," said the cat, again. He was not insistent. He was merely stating his decision. If Joth had ordered him to stay in the Underworld, he would probably have accepted the order. But in truth, Joth did not want to go back to his own world alone. He wanted Iorga's strength. It would be night in the Overworld now—he knew that because the camp was sleeping. If Iorga did not have to see the sun, why should the Overworld hold any particular terrors for him?

He said nothing. He opened the door, and they began to climb the stairs, together.

25.

"I think that you can help us," said Rypeck.

"I hope that I can tell you what you want to know," purred Sisyr.

Rypeck was sitting exactly as Warnet had sat, in the same chair. The expression of controlled politeness on his face was precisely the same. The faint sensation which he felt, of being imminently engaged in some kind of conflict, was precisely the same. Of all this, Rypeck remained, of course, completely unaware. Sisyr did not smile at the thought—if, in fact, the comparison was in his thoughts. Sisyr only smiled at human thoughts.

"What do you think of this so-called Second Euchronian Plan?" asked Rypeck.

"In what way?"

"Do you think it's practical?"

"Anything can be done, given the requisite time and the requisite determination," said Sisyr.

"Do we have those?"

"That is for you to decide," Sisyr pointed out.

Rypeck paused for a moment, wondering how to phrase a question so as to extract the kind of answer which he wanted.

"Do you think that the Plan will be a good thing for our society?" he asked.

"That, also, is for you to decide." said the alien, again.

"Do you believe that it will actually come to pass?" Rypeck tried again. "Will we actually manage to reclaim the Underworld?"

Now Sisyr hesitated. Finally, he said: "No."

Rypeck felt a slight surge of excitement. This was what he wanted to hear. This was what he wanted to know. There was no empirical reason why he should be pleased to discover that—in the opinion of the one person qualified to offer an opinion—the scheme would not succeed, but there was an undeniable element of pleasure in the brief sensation.

"It's been argued," said Rypeck, "that we have desperate need of a Plan. The heart of the Euchronian philosophy is Planning. Some people say that we should have begun a second Plan before we even finished the first. The Movement exists to Plan, they say. Euchronia exists to Plan. Each Millennium, they say, should be a beginning as well as an end."

"And what do you say?" asked the alien.

"I say: why? Why is the point of ends which are only beginnings? If the purpose of the first Plan was only to create the opportunity for a second Plan, would it ever have worked? I believe that the first Plan was successful only because it promised to deliver something real, solid, worthwhile and permanent. I believe that we should secure what we have made. I believe that the Second Plan is an exercise calculated to divert our attention from the real area of concern—which is the Overworld and Euchronian society. Perhaps we do need a Plan, but not this one. We need a Plan which will work with what we already have—

one which looks to the future. This Plan looks backwards in time. I don't like that."

Sisyr said nothing.

"Tell me," said Rypeck. "You were in very large measure responsible for the success of the first Euchronian Plan. Perhaps you had little enough to do with its ends, but you had everything to do with the means. Are you, then, a Euchronian? Did you believe in the Plan and what it was trying to accomplish?"

"In your terms," said the alien, "no."

Rypeck stared into the depths of his wineglass for a moment or so, while he digested the implications of that remark.

"I expected something exotic," he said, tilting the wineglass to show that he was referring to the wine. He was trying to fill in the gap before his next plunge into the esoteric realms of alien rationality.

"Wine from a distant star," said Sisyr, his voice deliberately conveying lightness and humor.

"Perhaps," said Rypeck. "Unusual, at any rate."

"Earth is my home," said Sisyr. "I live very much as you do."

"But you don't," countered Rypeck. "You don't live as we do. You live forever. You live outside our society, outside our terms of reference. Relative to Euchronia, you have objectivity. You can see what we do not in terms of our immediate future, or all the future we can reach in our imagination, but in terms of absolute time."

"There is no such thing," said the alien. "My view of your world is as subjective as your own. Mine is a different subjectivity, but it is formed in the same way: by experience. I have not lived through all of time. Even if I had, there is all of time still to come. I am not a man, but I am only an animal, just as a man is only an animal. I am sentient, as a man is sentient. I am not transient, but even a man is not ephemeral compared to those creatures which he has named the ephemerae. Are you objective enough to pronounce ultimate judgment on the destiny of the mayfly? Such a question is meaningless. What do you want to make of me? A god? Or simply the mouthpiece of a godly concept which you have, named Truth or Reason? There are no gods of the kind you want to make. There are realms beyond those you can perceive, beyond those you can imagine. But they are *real* realms, not quintessential dimensions superimposed upon your own. They are populated by real beings, living real lives, who are no less and no more relevant to your lives than you are to theirs.

"I do not know what kind of advice you want from me, my friend. I will tell you what I know in answer to any of your questions. But you must not try and make me into something I am not. You would not understand if I told you that I am only human, so I tell you that I am only animal. But I am forced to do so only because your concept of 'humanity' is so narrow."

Rypeck shook his head. "I'm sorry," he said, "but I can't think of you as 'only human.' I don't want to make you into a god, or a priest, or a seer, or a mouthpiece for some imaginary ultimate. But what you actually *are*—alien, immortal, enigmatic, knowing more than the whole human race knows—all this means that I cannot think of you as human."

Sisyr bowed his head. "I apologize," he said. "It is difficult. What you see in me, and what I see in you...there is little enough understanding between us. Forgive me. But please accept my answers to your questions. They are the answers I see, even though they are not answers as you see them. Please ask your questions."

Rypeck allowed a minute to drain past, emptying the air of confusion.

"Do you know what I mean by i-minus?" he asked.

"Yes."

"Please tell me. I...have to know that you know."

"It is the effect by which your Planners attempted to unify the Euchronian Movement when the Plan seemed endangered. By secret censorship of dreams and intensive propaganda in association they contrived to commit everyone involved in the movement to a single set of ideals and perspectives. The active propaganda became unnecessary very quickly—once it had 'taken' it was self-perpetuating. The agent to suppress what your scientists called the 'instinctive' input into dreams continued to be supplied. It still is. In order to control and monitor the administration of the drug the Planners laid down strict rules as to which persons and groups of persons were to know of its existence and purpose. As an executive body in charge of the secret itself they established a 'Close Council' to whom all those party to the secret would be responsible. You, I believe, were coopted into this Close Council on the death of one of its members shortly after you were elected to the Council sixty years ago."

"You seem to know more than I do," commented Rypeck.

"Probably," agreed Sisyr.

"I did not know that the Plan was endangered."

"It was never admitted. History is always subject to the most stringent censorship."

"You also seem less than certain about the operation of the agent. Are we wrong in believing that it controls the instinctive input into dreams, thereby short-circuiting the programming of instinctive behavior and response into the individual?"

"You are not wrong," said Sisyr. "But I do not see the process in quite those terms. What you understand as 'instinct' I understand in a rather different way. But it is merely a way of looking at things. Your conceptual model of the way that the brain works is no less real than mine."

Rypeck did not know quite how to interpret this statement.

"We believe," he said carefully, "that the i-minus agent secures social stability. I, personally, believe that its use should be discontinued because its presumed effects, as reflected in our everyday life, do not seem to me to be ultimately desirable. Heres, and others, argue that if it were not for the cohesive effect of the i-minus agent, our society might well begin to disintegrate entirely. I will not ask you whether you believe the agent to be beneficial, because you would not answer, but I ask you this: in your opinion, would the discontinuation of the i-minus project result in the de-stabilization of our society?"

"I will try to answer," said the alien, "but you must remember what I have already said. My answers are not necessarily yours. Your society is not stable. Change cannot be defeated, by any means whatsoever. In terms of the relative stability of your present situation, I would say that the i-minus effect is quite irrelevant. May I suggest—and this is merely a suggestion—that you consider the possibility that the apparent *need* for commitment to a new Plan is the legacy of the i-minus project."

Rypeck pondered that suggestion. It was not altogether new to him. But as an argumentative weapon, it was distinctly two-edged. As an argument against *both* the Second Plan and the i-minus project it was viable, but from the standpoint of someone committed to either, it would become an argument in favor of the other.

He began another line of inquiry.

"Suppose the Council were to approach you and ask for your help with respect to this Plan, just as they asked for your help with the old Plan. Would you give that help?"

"This time, my help is not needed," said Sisyr, ambiguously. "But I am always ready to help, in certain ways. There are kinds of help I cannot give, but my knowledge is always at the disposal of anyone who cares to ask."

Rypeck eyed the alien carefully. "Knowledge can be misused," he pointed out.

"Can it?" said Sisyr, blandly.

"If you favor one side in a conflict with knowledge which the other side does not possess, you give weight to that element of the conflict. However external you may be to the quarrel there remains an implicit judgment in your aid. You provide knowledge which supplements belief and morality. In a war, the side with your knowledge might win whereas under other circumstances it would have lost. Suppose the side which asked for your help were the aggressors? Suppose they used your knowledge to slaughter their enemies, or enslave them? Suppose both sides asked for your help, and you aided both, so that the result of the war, in terms of winning, was not altered, but that hundreds of thousands of people were killed, who need not have been had the warring parties not had access to the knowledge which made such slaughter possible?"

"For such help as I give," said Sisyr. "I accept the responsibility. The consequences of my actions have to be weighed—according to my standards and precepts. But what you describe as the possible consequences of action can, under other circumstances, be the consequences of inaction. My presence on Earth is a fact. When I am asked for help, I have to weigh the consequences of refusal as well as the consequences of agreement. According to my own morality. It is always possible—inevitable—that when some of you will judge me right, others will judge me wrong. In the end, only I can decide—but I cannot decide according to your criteria."

"I see," said Rypeck. "Then may I suggest—and this is only a suggestion—that you consider the following possibility. Neither Heres nor the Council will approach you for help with the Second Plan. They will see the Second Plan as an opportunity to accomplish something that is completely the work of the Euchronian Movement. They have claimed the credit for the first Plan, and perhaps that is right. They have excluded you from their history and their memory so far as is politic and practical. They do not want you in the Second Plan. They want to do without you, to prove to themselves that Euchronia is adequate.

"In this instance, therefore, we do not need to concern ourselves with the possibilities inherent in your action. What we do need to consider, however, are the possibilities inherent in your continued inaction. If you do nothing, then the i-minus project will continue, and the Second Plan will get under way. You have already said that you do not believe the Plan will succeed. The Underworld will not be reclaimed. We face failure, therefore. What would that do to our world? What is going to happen to both the Overworld and the Underworld if Heres' scheme marches forward to its failure? I offer these thoughts for your consideration. I do not ask you to intervene now, to further my aims or Euchronia's aims. I just ask you to think."

Sisyr nodded. Rypeck's suggestion was no more new to him than his had been to Rypeck.

"You know that the Underworld is lighted by electric stars?" said Rypeck, changing direction again.

"Yes," said Sisyr.

"You know that the Underworld is supplied with materials from the Overworld, somehow?"

"Yes."

"You know how?"

"Yes."

"No need to go into it now. I'll ask some other time. It's not important. Suppose that the Underworld doesn't want to be reclaimed. Suppose the Second Euchronian Plan becomes an all-out catastrophe. A conflict of motives. If Heres and the Council decide to reclaim the Underworld *in spite of* the Underworld, and it comes to war, who do you help? The Overworld, by inaction, or the Underworld, by intervention? What happens when Heres puts the stars out? Do you switch them on again, or do you let us destroy the Underworld before we can turn it into a garden? Just tell me that."

"I cannot see the future," said Sisyr, who appeared to be smiling. "And if I could, I am sure I would not see the kind of future that you see. I cannot decide on the kind of criteria by which you make your decisions. But I will say this. You think of two worlds, where I see only one. You have forgotten the Underworld, but it is still there, and whether you remember it or not, it is still a component of your past, your present, and your future. It is real. You have only rediscovered it in your imagination. Do not make the mistake of assuming that what you find *there* is real.

"I am not the only alien on Earth."

26.

Iorga looked up at the stars. The real stars, unsteady in the sky. He watched the racing clouds, which dressed and undressed the pockmarked face of the moon. He breathed the fresh, clean, cold air.

And he shivered.

Joth stood by the roadside and watched him, impassive but keenly observant.

He isn't overcome with awe or fear, thought Joth. Does he feel fear? Of course. But he knows fear. He lives in constant company with it. It is under control. It's a healthy fear. There's no trace of superstitious terror in him. He knows this world is real. What he sees, he can name, even if he can't understand. This is a savage, and perhaps an ignorant savage, but his mind isn't so limited. He knew this world was here, and he knew something of its nature. He isn't shocked. This is no challenge to his erstwhile understanding of the universe.

And yet, Joth's thoughts continued, this is his Heaven. This is what supplies, for him, the image of the other world. This is his Valhalla, his Olympus. Only it's not populated by gods and the spirits of the departed. Men live here. Ordinary men...and one or two with metal faces. He accepts even that. His world is a complex place—inherently strange enough to include men with steel faces...friends with steel faces. This world is real to him. Strange, but not alien. In prehistoric times, when the farmers came to the city, when the poor invaded the land of the rich, or the rich the realms of the poor, they may have felt as he feels now.

Alone and afraid, but still entombed in reality. In a world unknown, but knowable. Genuine.

Joth's interpretation of Iorga's feelings was, perhaps, accurate enough. Iorga could not have discovered words to give an alternative account. But Joth could not really know. He could understand, but only according to his own way of seeing. In the final analysis, his analogies were limited, as all analogies are.

"We must hurry," said Joth. "There's not enough time left to do what we must tonight, so we have to find shelter for the day. A hiding place. If the people down below alert Harkanter, that's too bad. I hope they won't. Either way, if I can get to a public phone I'll requisition transport from the net. We'll go home. You can lie up in a dark room, and I can get a doctor for my back. After nightfall, we go find Camlak."

Iorga signaled his agreement without speaking.

"If the sun comes up," said Joth, "shield your eyes. If you look at it you'll be blinded."

Iorga nodded again.

Joth balanced the two guns which he had stolen from Rath in his two hands.

"You take the pistol," he said. "You know how it works?"

"No."

"That's a catch to stop it firing. Keep it sealed until you want to use the gun. Then release it, point the barrel, and press the trigger. Be careful. Don't shoot unless someone points one at you. It shouldn't be necessary to kill anyone. I don't want anyone to get hurt. All right?"

They moved off together, away from the plexus and into the night.

27.

Randal Harkanter shook hands all around. There were a lot of hands to shake. He had invited a lot of people to his little surprise.

Vicente Soron fluttered round like a butterfly, nervous and excited. No one in the crowd knew who he was. Nobody cared. All eyes were on Harkanter, the man with charisma.

Among the guests, it was Yvon Emerich who naturally assumed the lead. Of all the people there he was the only one used to real crowds. For gathering in this fashion was not customary. People who live their lives by courtesy of machines gradually become...sensitive...to the proximity of large quantities of flesh. It seems unnatural. But Emerich knew the small skills of organizing crowds in order to keep uneasiness at bay. His aide, Alwyn Ballow, was a tower of strength in his support.

There was one member of the Council present—Javan Sobol—but the Euchronian Movement was conspicuously underrepresented relative to prominent anti-Euchronians. Sobol had observed this discrepancy within minutes, but he read nothing into it. Harkanter was not popular with the average Hoh-playing, propriety-observing Euchronians. Sobol had no idea what Harkanter planned to show them, but it did not occur to him for a moment that it might be a revelation which intimately concerned Council decisions. Joel Dayling, who considered himself the leader of the Eupsychian opposition to the Council, was equally unaware of the nature and magnitude of the planned surprise. Harkanter, who slotted naturally and comfortably into the role of showman, had given out no hints, except perhaps to Ballow, who needed some leverage in order to make sure that Yvon Emerich would be sufficiently interested to turn up.

"You didn't stay long downstairs," said Emerich to his host, loud enough for anyone interested to hear. "What brought you back? Or sent you back? Have you had a revelation like Magner's?"

"In a manner of speaking," Harkanter answered.

"Then you've come to propose marriage," said Emerich. "Tell us, please, whether Euchronia is to be the bride or the groom?" Emerich was being deliberately trivial and inane. He liked to appear something of the eccentric, something of the clown, in his private *persona.* He believed it necessary to retain what he saw as his real self (incisive, brilliant and destructive) for "his" public, who met him only through the medium of their holovisual pseudoreality. He was their idol and their champion—his facade was theirs, packaged and distributed by the machine.

"If what you have to say concerns the Underworld," said

Sobol, "I'm not sure that we'd rather not hear it. We've heard far too much of late, and we'd have been perfectly pleased if your little party down there had gone on for a year or two before coming back to bore us with all the latest news from Tartarus."

"That will be heresy this time next week," Dayling intervened. "Now we have a Second Euchronian Plan any negative thought regarding the Underworld will be anti-Euchronian. If I were you, Javan, I'd be careful what I said. You might end up driving a tractor instead of running the world."

"It will all be done by remote control," said Sobol. "This isn't the age of psychosis. We have the resources of the Cybernet behind us. The machines will roll out of the factories and into the Underworld, and they'll all be controlled by a handful of men in a handful of control rooms. There will have to be a few men to go down to ground level, but I assure you that no one will need to get their hands dirty. It will all go very smoothly. It won't take ten thousand years, either. I wouldn't be at all surprised if some of us live to see the job nearly done."

For the most part, the speech fell on deaf ears. Most of the audience deserted him before he closed, and independent conversation sprang up in two or three places. One man, however, could not resist pointing out to Sobol the error of his assumptions. That was Vicente Soron. Ironically, he was one of the few people in the gathering who were actually more dedicated to Euchronia than the councillor himself.

"Javan," said Soron, in a low voice, "there isn't going to be a Second Euchronian Plan. You don't understand."

"Nonsense," said Sobol, whose faith in Heres was implicit.

"It's all a terrible mistake," said Soron, the intensity of his voice making little impact on his listener's conviction. "A terrible mistake. You'll see...."

He drifted off, carried away by a current of movement which began as Harkanter ended the preliminaries and led the group into another room. Here there was room for them to sit, while Harkanter explained. They did so, arranging themselves most carefully. Emerich sat off to one side, and Sobol was content to stay back. Lesser individuals were permitted to gather at the big man's feet. Dayling sat in the center, staring Harkanter full in the face. He wondered what it was all about. Harkanter seemed to be building up to a trick of some kind—a big joke. He could practically see the laugh poised in Harkanter's throat. Knowing the big man as he did, Dayling wondered who that laugh was going to hurt.

Harkanter began to tell them about his experiences in the Underworld. He was by no means an orator, and his descriptive powers were decidedly poor, but he rushed at his story with evident enthusiasm, and those present were prepared to bear with him for a while.

He was vague about the results of Rath's work in surveying the territory, principally because he had not waited for the results to turn up anything worthwhile. He left out the matter of the mysterious grave altogether. He concentrated on his own viewpoint and his own actions, and he succeeded in giving the impression that the whole Underworld was a gigantic polluted swamp teeming with crabs and less pleasant life-forms of lowly and loathsome nature.

He set out on a description of his walk with Soron, which Soron found to be somewhat embarrassing, and then he gave a wordy account of his own lack of good sense in getting himself stuck in the mud.

Then he paused. Knowing it was for effect, the crowd waited politely.

"It was then," concluded Harkanter, "that we found what we were really looking for."

There was no doubt in anyone's mind that he was referring to the much-discussed people of the Underworld.

"He came out of the bushes," said Harkanter, "with a dagger the length of my forearm. I was helpless—the gun was in the mud with me and if I fired it I was as likely to get killed as he was. But Vicente was magnificent. Up like a cat, with his gun in hand. One shot—all it took. Full in the chest. Went down all in a heap and never raised a finger again. Then Vicente went off like a hare to get the men out of camp to drag me out of the mudhole and cart the carrion home. Only it's not carrion. It's alive. And it's here."

The silence did not last long.

"Here?" said Emerich. "You mean, in the house."

"I brought him back," said Harkanter. "I thought you all ought to get a look at him. A good, long look. It will tell you better than I, or any man, could tell you the truth about the Underworld."

"Now wait a minute," said Sobol. "You can't...."

But Harkanter was already leading the way down to the cellars of his house.

28.

Camlak was in a cage surrounded by screens. He had been shot full of sedatives half a dozen times since Soron had first knocked him out. Soron had been unable to estimate the dosage with much accuracy, and had been prepared to overdo things rather than run any risks. Camlak felt that he was not quite wearing his body. His mind was so sluggish that the hands on the clock on the wall, which he could just see over the top of the screens, and which was the only feature of the room accessible to his eyes, seemed to be moving very quickly indeed. He felt as if he were wholly immersed in a viscous liquid, and stretched out over a large area, yet not drawn taut. His mouth was bone dry and he felt infinitely heavy. He had been given neither food nor water since he had first been taken.

His eyes were open but they seemed to be stuck that way. He could see, but he was unable to focus his attention or withdraw his stare. The hands of the clock held his gaze absolutely.

That was *time*. Time passing. He knew.

He felt an odd echo somewhere inside himself, as though the knowledge was highly significant.

He heard the clatter of many pairs of feet coming down the

stairway, but it seemed like a distant rumble, unimportant and irrelevant. In many parts of the Underworld, he knew, one could hear an omnipresent whisper which indicated the working of machinery above the sky. It was one of those things that had to be blotted out of consciousness. Real, but without meaning.

Then the screens were snatched away dramatically, and he was exposed, naked and only half alive, to the shocked stare of the people of the Overworld.

The suddenness of it was a dull jerk in his mind, to which he tried very hard to react, but he could neither move nor alter the direction of his stare. He tried to speak, but he was quite incapable of it. Only a hollow rattle passed his lips as the breath oozed out of his throat.

"I have to tell you," Randal Harkanter was saying to his guests, in a loud and commanding voice, "that the 'people' of the Underworld—the only *people* of the Underworld—are *giant rats!*"

29.

The sun was rising just as Joth came home.

He indicated that Iorga should follow closely, and they went upstairs, quietly and carefully. No stealth was necessary, and he could not have explained why it came so naturally to him. But at present, even within his own home, the Overworld seemed to be a strange and unfamiliar place. He had entered it an invader, covertly.

He found his own room empty and he told Iorga to stay there. The windows were screened and only thin lines of light filtered through. Iorga would find it safe enough, if not exactly comfortable. The cat's eyes continually moved around the room, as if they felt the solidity of the walls and the perfect angularity of its construction. Unlike the Men Without Souls and the Children of the Voice, the Hellkin were not town-dwellers but nomads, who found natural shelter preferable to the crude brick and chitinous lath which provided basic material for virtually all Underworld builders.

The eyes were the only betrayal of Iorga's unease. He still moved with perfect balance and grace, he still said nothing. But inside himself, he had never felt more alone. That was particularly bad for him, because he belonged to a race which did not court loneliness, like the Cuchumanates, and possessed no foil against it, as did the Children of the Voice. A rat could never be alone while he held inside himself the access to the being which he called his Gray Soul. But if the cats had such souls, they had found no way to reach and commune with them.

Joth went into his sister's room. She was there, asleep, alone in the house. Her face on the pillow was not peaceful. How could it be? For her, this house must now be filled with ghosts. Her long-dead mother she would not remember, but Ryan and Joth, and finally her father, had all been taken from her, one after the other, in relentless succession. She had been the agent of Joth's disappearance—at least in her own mind, and the witness to her father's murder. She did not need instinct to be frightened by what she found in her dreams. She was haunted.

Joth would not have been surprised to find the house empty and deserted, with Julea gone. Why had she stayed? What was there here to hold her except memory and misery?

It was an easy answer. She was waiting. Waiting, perhaps without hope, because she had to wait. Because she did not know, for sure, that all the ghosts were the ghosts of the dead.

The ghost reached out to switch on the lamp beside the bed, turning down its intensity so that it became a dull yellow glow. He did not need to adjust his own eyes, once he had reduced the intensity. He had not yet seen the sun.

Julea awoke, her eyes flying to the light switch, and she saw Joth. Though his body and his clothing were beyond recognition his metal face stood out starkly clear as his one most meaningful feature. She knew him immediately, but she did not scream. Perhaps she had seen him hours, or even minutes, before, while she slept. The shock seemed to come slowly, but it struck deep into her, and paralyzed her body. Tears came to the corners of her eyes, but they did not fall. There was a brief period of silence, which seemed to both of them to be very long.

In the end of the silence, deep in the well of her emotions, there was utter turmoil. She did not know what to feel or to believe.

"I'm all right," said Joth, in a whisper. "I wasn't killed. I found my way back. Just take it easy."

He waited for her reply. He could have said more, but he wanted to hear her voice before he went on. The sight of her, haloed by the reflected gleam of the dim light, had reminded him that he had come back to his beginning, that this was his world, and that this was where he belonged, if he belonged anywhere.

"I thought you were dead," she said.

"Ryan's dead," he told her. "Our father died, too. I saw him die."

"So did I," she whispered.

He accepted the statement without surprise. He knew what she meant.

"But we were in different worlds," he said. Then, after a pause: "It isn't Hell. Sometimes we can come back. It's only another world."

"You're hurt," she said. Her voice was strangely cold and metallic. But she was no longer whispering, and the tautness was leaving her body.

"That's right," he said. "I want you to call a doctor. But don't tell him why. Just tell him to come."

"Why?"

"I don't want any record of my return to go into the cybernet. I requisitioned transport by remote. No voice. No one can know I'm here, yet. I want it to stay that way."

"The doctor...."

"He won't tell anyone. If I ask him not to. It doesn't matter so much about people—it's the net that I'm worried about. Once the net has the information, it's there for anyone to recall."

She said nothing, but she was searching his face with her eyes. She thought—she had always thought—that even the metal and the false flesh could contain meaning. But she could find nothing, and her face was clouded with uncertainty.

"It's all right," he said, gently. "There's something that I have to do, first. I'm not going back, I promise you. When I've done what I came to do, I'll declare myself. But for now, for today and tonight, I don't want anyone to know I'm here.

"If anyone asks," he added, remembering Rath, "then deny that you've seen me. I'll keep out of range of the decks and the holographic units."

She didn't understand.

"Just call the doctor," said Joth. "The quicker he gets to me, the sooner I can get my back patched up."

Julea got out of bed and dressed slowly. Then they went downstairs together, and Joth waited while his sister put a call through from the central unit to the doctor. Julea only had to ask him to come. He was ready enough to jump to the conclusion that she was in need of attention. He knew that she had been alone in the house for some time, and the unfortunate circumstances of her loneliness.

"I've got to clean myself up," said Joth. "I've been like this for so long I just don't get any dirtier. I must stink."

She followed him upstairs again, and into the bathroom. She helped him peel off the remnants of his clothing, and she removed the makeshift bandage which concealed and protected the greater part of the vast open wound on his back. She felt sickened by the ugliness of the tormented flesh, but she tried hard not to react.

He could not lie down in the bath, and he could not bear the direct impact of the hot water. She began to sponge him with lukewarm water, without soap.

"What happened?" she asked, faintly, not knowing whether or not she wanted to know.

"I followed Burstone. I went down to take a look around. He cut me off. Lifted the cage and left me stranded. I've been there...how long have I been there?"

"Months," she said.

"Like years," he murmured. "I've aged years."

"How did you live?"

He laughed, quietly. The laughter was forced. "One lives," he said. "It's easy. You just go on. You start out alive and you just carry straight on. They made me live...but how? I don't know how. I ate dirt, I breathed foul air, I drank foul water. And I just kept going, through all the fevers and the pains. I don't know the way. I just kept on. They brought me through."

"The people of the Underworld?"

"The people. The men in Hell."

"How did this happen?" She was referring to the wound.

"Never mind," he told her. "It doesn't matter."

"It must hurt terribly."

"It hurts," he told her, flatly. "But there comes a time when things hurt and you just say 'so what.' Things hurt. Life hurts, down there. You live with it."

"The book," she said. "It was all true. The dreams told the truth."

"The dreams...yes, the dreams told the truth. The dreams were real. But the book—that wasn't true. He couldn't understand, you see. What he saw was just a confused mess of images, what he felt was just a boiling sea of feeling. Everything all mixed up. He couldn't entangle it, because he didn't understand. He couldn't. There was no way. The book is a mistake, Julea. It's their world. It *does* hurt, but it's their world. We can't open it to the sun. We've masked the Face of Heaven, just as he said, but the mask has become the face. There's no other face, so far as they're concerned. He didn't understand what's happened down there in ten thousand years. They have a new world of their own. They're new people. The men on the ground that *he* believed in don't exist. There are no people like us—just people *unlike* us. Whatever we do about the Underworld, it will be an invasion. There's nothing we *can* do, except keep to the world we have made for ourselves. That's what I'll have to make them understand...afterwards."

"After what?"

"Our father," he said, oblivious to her remark, following his own train of thought, "wanted to be a saint. He wanted to open up the old world as if it were the same as ever, entombed and waiting, ripe for resurrection. He wanted to go down there, a saint from Heaven to forgive and reclaim the condemned of Hell. Don't you see that the book is about *him*, not about them? They have no need of saints. The living can't be resurrected. There may be a hundred or a thousand doors to the Underworld, but it doesn't matter whether they're open or shut. Not to us, not to them. There are two worlds. Alive, different, touching. Nothing can change that. The doors can't be used. Not really."

"You used one," she said. "Burstone uses one. Back and forth, many times. Ryan said so."

"For nothing," Joth said. "It's all pointless. A thousand years ago...five thousand years ago...the job that Burstone does meant something. Not any more. The world is new. Burstone's a relic—a vestige of something that was once worthwhile but is now useless. I used a door, but it didn't make a difference. Not a meaningful difference. Camlak came through, too, but that won't mean anything either."

"Camlak?"

"A friend. My friend."

"A man from the Underworld?"

"That's right."

"I don't understand."

"Neither do I. No one can."

"Is that what you have to do? Find your friend?"

"And take him back. In the long run, it makes no difference, but for his sake. For the sake of his child. I have to undo all the trouble my father caused. I have to make sure the Underworld is left alone."

"They're going to reclaim it," she said.

"What!"

"The Hegemon announced a second Plan. We can't bring the

people of the Underworld up here, so we're going to remake their world. Like ours."

"They don't know what they're doing," he whispered.

"No," she said.

There was silence. His skin was clean—relatively. He was drying himself gently, trying desperately not to tear the skin where it was scabbed and scratched.

Julea stood up. "I'll get you some clean clothes."

She was halfway into the corridor when he shouted "No!"

"What's the matter?" she asked.

"In my room...."

Her eyes opened wide. She was staring at him. From where she stood she could see all of his naked body, ravaged by the Underworld. It looked completely out of place in the clean, smooth environment which surrounded it. Everything was neat, everything shaped perfectly, surfaced brightly, angled precisely. Joth had brought into it the filth and the ugliness of elsewhere. For a fleeting instant, he seemed, himself, to be a kind of wound. A living scar.

"There's one of them here," she said. "A man from the Underworld."

Joth did not dare to nod or shake his head.

He said: "It's not *exactly* a man."

30.

When Joachim Casorati arrived Joth was downstairs, lying full-length on a couch, face downwards. He was still unclothed, but his body was covered by a large towel.

The doctor stared at him for some moments.

"Joth," he said, finally. His tone was neutral. It was almost a formal greeting. He had defeated both his surprise and his curiosity, for the time being.

"Joachim," Joth returned the greeting. "I want you to dress some wounds. Some may need cleaning out, if there's danger of infection. I'll need some shots, but don't give me anything which will put me to sleep or slow me down. I can't wait to be put back together inch by inch. Patch me up so I work. That's all."

The doctor lifted up the towel to look at Joth's back, and then flipped back the edge to expose the big wound.

"What did this?" he asked.

"A surgeon with a knife," said Joth.

"A surgeon," repeated the doctor, blankly.

"An amateur," Joth told him. "It needed doing. I was growing something nasty and it had to be taken out. The operation was a success, the patient lived, but the healing was slow."

"I can't patch that up," said the doctor. "You need two weeks in a medical unit. How long have you been walking around in this condition? You could have died."

"You know where I've been," said Joth.

"The Underworld."

"I hadn't any choice but to walk around, just as I had no choice about the butchering."

"Did Harkanter find you?"

"No."

"Does anyone know you're back? Does anyone know where you've been?"

"No. And I don't want them to know. I'll explain it to you later. Not today, but someday soon. You'll have your chance to reassemble me. But I can't talk now. Patch me up so that I can keep going for a couple more days. Don't ask me any more questions now. All right?"

The doctor shook his head. "It's not all right," he said. He knelt to examine the wounds with his eyes and his fingers. Joth winced at every touch, but did not cry out.

Casorati removed the towel altogether and looked at the abrasions on Joth's legs. Once or twice he looked more closely at specific injuries.

"I've had feelers out from the Council," commented the doctor. "About you. About your father. About your ancestry and every bug you've picked up in twenty years. They're very interested in you."

"The Council?"

"Somebody on the Council. I don't know what they wanted because I couldn't tell them."

"Don't tell them I'm back. Not yet."

Casorati shook his head again. "This is going to take time," he said. "If I do what you want I'll have to put plastic on your shoulder and back. If you wait, we can restore it. You'll lose some of the use of your left arm if I patch it. You've got enough plastic already, Joth. I don't want to put any more on if I can help it. You'll regret it later if I do. You'll have to live a hundred years with a bad arm, unless you let it heal properly."

"I want it patched."

"I'll have to requisition equipment."

"Just don't mention my name."

"What's it all for? The secrecy, the cloak-and-dagger game?"

"It's important. Requisition your equipment. How long will it take?"

"Could be hours. I'll have to give you antibiotics for some of these infections. If I dress all the wounds you'll have gel all over you."

"Just do it," said Joth. "Please."

31.

"A rat?" said Warnet, incredulously.

"That's right," Dayling told him. "We all saw it. It was a rat all right. But what a rat! More than four feet long. With *hands*— tiny, but real. And Harkanter showed us the knife. Some weapon! Emerich was there, and ten or fifteen others. The only councillor was Sobol, but by now the news will be all through the Movement. Heres must be sweating. This has ruined him. His precious speech making Magner a martyr has made an absolute fool of him. When Emerich gets on the air tonight Heres will be dead and buried, politically. If we petition for an election now we're made. The platform is already cut and dried."

"Exterminate the vermin," said Warnet, drily.

"Of course."

"Don't."

Dayling reached out and grasped the younger man by the arm. Warnet recoiled slightly from the violation, but did not shake off the grip.

"This is it," he insisted. "There's going to be a wave of hysteria rippling all round the world tonight. Into every home in the world. Emerich is recording right now. He took film of the specimen while we were there last night, and he was interviewing Harkanter in the early hours. All day he'll be putting together a broadcast that will rock Euchronia on its stilts. This is our chance."

"No, Joel," said Warnet. "You don't understand. You've missed the point. Harkanter has made a mistake. You want to rush headlong after Heres. Don't you see? Heres jumped the gun, and you want to do exactly the same. We *don't know* about the Underworld. A rumor here, a specimen there, a compendium of chopped logic and uninspired guesses...can't you see how inadequate it all is? What sort of conclusions can we draw? If someone came up here and kidnapped a street cleaner would they conclude that nothing exists here except machines? Think about what you're doing, Joel. We need more information."

"We need to hit Heres," Dayling retorted. "Someone has to be prepared to go up against him now and make him out a fool and a traitor to the whole human race. He has to be obliterated. If we sit back and wait for more information, he'll regroup. He'll revise all his ideas and come out with more talk by the mile, and while time drags by he'll get himself out of it. Even if his head rolls do you think the Movement can't afford to lose him? *We* have to act now. *We* have to lead the attack. It's the best chance we'll ever have. Maybe the only chance. We'd be fools to lose it."

Warnet would not agree. "We'd be fools to commit ourselves.

We already know better than that. We know full well that Harkanter has his facts cockeyed. Burstone wasn't trading with any rats. Sisyr was talking about humans. They *know*. Harkanter doesn't. If we start howling for the sealing of the Underworld we could run right into a trap. Heres will shift his ground. We know that. All right, where to? I'll tell you where—he'll say that Harkanter's find makes our intervention in the Underworld all the more necessary. He'll say that it is our duty to save the people of the Underworld from the menace of the rats."

"But that's just it," said Dayling. "Emerich is going on the air tonight to show that the so-called people of the Underworld *are* rats. That's Harkanter's claim!"

"Joel, he's *wrong*."

"The world doesn't know that."

"It soon will. Once Harkanter's through with his big show, what then? Do you think Burstone and others like him will sit still while this stupid lie is broadcast? What about the scientists down below? The ones who are *really* trying to find out what the Underworld is like?"

"*Then* will be later," Dayling persisted. "We can smash the Movement—the Council, at least—right *now*."

"For the sheer pleasure of breaking it? Do you think you'd last a day longer than the man you displaced when the truth finally comes out?"

"What do *you* propose?"

"That we adopt the course no one else can. We criticize Heres for rushing his fences. We criticize Harkanter for rushing *his*. We plead for sweet reason and time. We place ourselves in the right. In the long term, that will be far better for us than any panic-buying we can do now."

"Half the Euchronians will take exactly the same stance. What advantage is there in doing exactly what they do?"

Warnet paused for a moment. He took time out to dislodge Dayling's hand from his forearm. "I'm not sure that they will," he said. "Heres is in deep. He can't play for time now. He's spent all his. And the others...it seems to me they're far more likely to take Harkanter's evaluation of the situation at face value than we are. Most of them will *want* to believe it—they never wanted the Underworld to be resurrected at all. I think the Council might well go over like a pendulum and vote to seal it up forever. I think they may fight more bitterly between themselves than we ever thought possible."

"But if you're wrong...," said Dayling.

32.

"We're getting deeper into trouble every minute," said Rypeck. "We've got to start pulling ourselves out now. This situation has complicated itself far too rapidly, thanks to Rafael's supposed masterstroke. I've tried to call him and he's just not available."

"We can ride out this ridiculous affair," said Acheron Spiro confidently. "Who listens to Emerich?"

"About half the world."

"Yes, but not the *Movement*. You've got to remember, Eliot, that the Movement is much bigger than this kind of scare-mongering. We work on a much vaster scale. We've had these waves of hysteria before, on a smaller scale, and none of them has amounted to anything. They pass, Eliot, they pass."

Rypeck swore silently. He felt like screaming at the other man's complacency.

"In the wider context, the problem is just the same," said Spiro, attempting to explain. "What we are facing is a loss of faith. This rumor about the rats is simply another symptom of it. The people have no *direction*. This is what Rafael's trying to give them. He's trying to give them a goal—a new vision."

"It's the vision of a blind man," said Rypeck. "I've tried to convey to all of you that we are abysmally ignorant as regards the true state of affairs, not only in the Underworld but in *our* world. The *real* reason that Rafael has embarked upon this idiot crusade on behalf of the Underworlders is purely and simply to evade the question of the i-minus agent."

"It's *irrelevant*, Eliot."

"It's not dead simply because Magner has been removed from the arena of decision. He may not have been the only one. There may be ten or ten thousand. We have to find out."

"This is an old argument, Eliot. I've heard it all before. Why did you call me?"

"I called you to suggest to you that it's time to pull out. It's time to leave Heres on his own and go our separate way."

"Who is *we*?"

"To begin with, the members of the Close Council. Enzo will be willing, and so—I think—will Clea. Dascon we don't need—he'd go down with Heres in any case. Sobol is already creating chaos outside the Close Council, and if we provide him with a base he'll come to us, and drag two-thirds of the Council with him."

"And what is this action supposed to achieve?" said Spiro, obviously unsympathetic.

"We call for a referendum on the Underworld question. We disassociate ourselves from Heres' statement in Council. We reject his Second Plan completely."

"And do...we...have any ideas of our own to propose as an alternative?"

"The cure of our own society. Isn't that our real aim? The abandonment of i-minus. A reexamination of the status quo. We don't need a second Euchronian Plan, because the *first* one hasn't yet been brought to its conclusion. That's our platform."

"You can't. It would be tantamount to undeclaring the Millennium. That's ridiculous."

"No, Acheron. It's necessary. It's vital. The Millennium, as we have called it, is a failure. It's a setback to the Plan. We must reinterpret and rethink. The *real* Millennium is not yet come. We have to face that. Rafael never could and never will."

"What makes you think that I could be persuaded to have anything to do with such a platform?" said Spiro. "If it comes to a struggle for power and support between you and Rafael, you can't win. Surely you must see that. No matter what sort of a tremor Emerich starts tonight you can't think that Rafael will be beaten. He has loyal support, Eliot, and you can count me in with that loyal support. What's more, I don't believe that Enzo and Clea will support you, either. There's no way you can get a majority of the Close Council. No way."

"That's the way you feel now, Acheron. All right. But you tune in to Emerich tonight and you watch the wind blowing. It'll blow a scare into you, Acheron. You can be sure of that. And one more thing...."

"Well?"

"If Heres goes...and go he will...we'll be needing a new Hegemon. He'd have to come from the Close Council, Acheron. I don't want the job. You bear that in mind, Acheron...Enzo and Clea aren't yet sixty, and *I don't want the job.*"

33.

They had to take Julea with them. She did not want to go, and Joth would have liked to leave her behind, but it was imperative that they should be admitted to Harkanter's house. Julea could identify herself at the door and it would be opened to her. Joth could not be sure that the same would hold true for him. Even if Harkanter had not been warned by Rath, he would recognize the metal face, and he would want to know why Joth was alive and well, in the Overworld, and knocking at his door.

Julea was frightened. Paradoxically, she was frightened not so much by Iorga as by Joth. Iorga she took more or less at face value—he was strange, but in no way hostile. He was not loathsome to look at, and he said and did nothing to inspire fear in her. But Joth was different. She feared the new Joth because he did not match her image of the old. Joth had gone into the Underworld a man of Euchronia, her brother—despite his mental face he had been the least alien of beings. But the Joth who had returned was measurably distant from her. Though he assumed sufficient familiarity to stand naked before her, he did not show that familiarity in his speech or his actions. There was no *rapport* between them as they talked. The things he said, and the way which he said them, were strange to her, and he made no apparent effort to draw her into his understanding. He spoke to her as he might speak to a stranger, or someone more than strange. They had lost their point of contact. Their mutual understanding counted for nothing, now. The life they had shared had withered inside him, and the life he was living now was something apart. For the first time in her life, Julea thought of the steel face as a mask, and wondered what might lie behind it.

The long drive through the night reminded her, inevitably, of the night when Abram Ravelvent had taken her father and herself to the lonely plexus through which the staircase to the Underworld descended. The parallel between the memories added to her inner disturbance. She was glad when the destination was finally reached, but her gladness came mixed with a rush of new anxieties as she wondered what might happen now.

She identified herself at the door, and gave as her reason for presenting herself the eminently credible story that she had come to see if Harkanter knew anything about her father, who had gone into the Underworld by the same door. The intensely personal nature of the inquiry offered some sort of excuse for her presenting herself in the flesh rather than making contact *via* the cybernet.

Harkanter unsealed the door for her without question. Joth and Iorga had kept well back from the range of the door's eye, but when the eye blinked and the door yielded, they hurried forward to pass through with the girl.

Joth felt good, for the first time in a virtual eternity. His flesh had been repaired with plastic, he was clean and properly clothed, and the possible depressant effect of the antibiotics he had taken were offset by a metabolic stimulator. He felt fast, and alert, and fully alive.

Iorga was wearing black eyeshades which Joth had modified for him. Outside, in the night, he did not need them, but Harkanter's house would be full of blazing light, and the cat needed protection from that.

The room into which they came was large and furnished according to a rather bizarre conglomeration of tastes. There was a great staircase and a balcony. The curtains which decked the windows instead of screens were lush and heavy, colored wine-red. The walls were lavishly decorated with artificially aged designs in metal and smoked glass. The atmosphere of the place was anachronistic, but the release from present time was confused and ill made. It was not a scene from the prehistoric past, but a montage of ideas reflecting wholly imaginary pasts in jigsawed association.

Harkanter chose to make his appearance on the balcony. On coming through the door, Joth and Iorga had stepped sideways into an alcove in the vestibule, and were not visible from the place where Harkanter stood. Julea, however, went forward into the room. She was nervous, and her steps were tentative.

Harkanter was puzzled by her apparent trepidation, and when she caught sight of him and looked up he knew that something was wrong. But he was still thinking of the grave and wondering what—and how—to tell her what he believed. He moved to the head of the stairs, useless phrases flowing through his mind.

"I'm very sorry," he said. "I had not expected...." He left the sentence hanging, deliberately, but he could see that she was not going to answer. She was not going to say anything. She was waiting, with incipient terror in her eyes. The big man had begun to come down the stairs, but he stopped, suddenly. He curled the fingers of his left hand so that the tips scraped sweat from the palm.

Joth stepped out of the alcove. He was not carrying the rifle, and the pistol was not visible. There was nothing about his appearance, save for his face, which seemed immediately strange, but Harkanter could almost feel his hostility.

"Who are you?" the big man demanded.

"Joth Magner."

There was a moment's silence. Harkanter showed no evidence of surprise.

"I didn't know," said the Negro, finally. "I heard that you were dead. I didn't see you at the door."

"No."

Harkanter continued his descent. "You want to know about your father?" he said.

"I know about my father," Joth told him. "I buried him."

Harkanter continued coming down the stairs. When he reached the bottom he came forward three or four paces to stand facing Joth. They were ten or twelve feet apart.

"Then what do you want from me?" he asked, quietly.

"Why did you bring him back?" asked Joth.

"Your father?"

"No. You know who I mean. The man you captured in the Underworld."

"That wasn't a man," said Harkanter. "It was a rat. I brought it back to show the people what the inhabitants of the Underworld are really like."

"And you showed them. A rat. Did you let him speak?"

"I don't know what you mean."

"I don't know what you told Emerich," said Joth, "but it wasn't true. We've been keeping in touch with the holovisual network. They've released nothing yet, except hints. But I know that whatever you've told them is a handful of lies, and I think you know it too."

"I showed them the rat," said Harkanter blandly. "They were all free to draw their own conclusions."

"His name is Camlak," said Joth, "and he's a man."

"Vicente Soron and the science of biology say it's a rat," Harkanter insisted. "We have proof."

"So have I," said Joth. He motioned with his hand. Iorga came out of the alcove. The cat was carrying the rifle. He was quite relaxed, but he was holding the weapon in a manner which suggested unmistakably that he knew how to use it.

Harkanter stood very still for a long time. Iorga stood as tall as he, and the shaded eyes stared into his own with calm self-consciousness. But Harkanter did not see a man. He saw a caricature, a travesty. He saw a beast stood erect, clothed and armed. He read viciousness and bestiality in the face. He saw cunning, but not intellect. He saw a big cat, no more.

The last thing that Harkanter had envisaged was the Underworld extending its claws into the Overworld in order to take him to task for drugging and caging the rat. While he stood and stared, he still considered his world as inviolate—*the* world. He still considered the Underworld as a sewer, a dark hole filled with vermin. That was what he believed. His belief could not be shaken by what he saw. He could not react to Iorga's presence. There was no way that he could. Iorga and the rifle were beyond his conceptual boundaries.

"We want Camlak," said Joth.

There was no reply.

"The man you call a rat. We want him. We want to take him back."

Still no reply.

Julea, very faintly, said: "Please."

Harkanter looked at the girl. He was glad to have his attention distracted.

"It's a rat," said Harkanter, with all the force of Vicente Soron's word of scientific honor behind him.

"Just show us where you have him," said Joth. "That's all. Take us to him. We'll take care of him then."

Harkanter wanted to be stubborn, but when he turned the idea over in his mind he realized that he had no stake in the matter. The rat had fulfilled his purpose. He had played his game. He did not want the rat. Not now.

"Take him," said Harkanter. "And welcome."

He turned and led the way down to the cellars. Joth and Iorga followed. Julea, after a moment's hesitation, went after them.

Vicente Soron moved back from the door at which he had been eavesdropping, and called the police.

34.

Camlak was drowning.

The oceanic swell of the drug was passing a gloved hand through his face, the fingers dragging at the mind behind the eyes, trying to claw him out of himself and spread him like a thin sliver of sunlit water on a pebble beach. It was trying to smear him into a thin sheet of egoic slime, and he felt inside himself that he was gradually melting into malleability. He was having difficulty holding himself together. The cohesive forces joining mind and brain were decaying and denaturing. He had already lost the sensations of gravity and heat to the counteractive gentleness of the drug. Soon, he knew, the force of identity would ebb away. The molecules of his mind would fly apart, their integrity ripped as if by a relentless tide, wrecked, disintegrating like a loose bundle of cotton threads. His being was no longer a knot, merely a tangle.

"Am I going to die?" he asked his Gray Soul.

The Soul was a shadow, a patch of darkness on the sun-spun sheen of his slithering thoughts. It was shaped like a dart or a moth at rest. It was steady, but it appeared to waver and ripple because of the pressure that was rippling his consciousness.

"No," replied the Soul. "You won't die."

"Must I keep fighting?" asked Camlak.

"Yes."

Camlak did as he was advised. He kept fighting. But he still felt that he was losing the fight. He still felt that he was being dissolved into the thin, shallow waves, diffusing into the liquid layers of the drug which reached for him from the well of his bloodstream.

He trusted the Soul. He could see the Soul, and while he knew the Soul was there he knew that there was a chance for him to reverse the process of disintegration that was extinguishing him.

But he did not quite know how.

He struggled alone, in the abyss, for an eternity, while the molecules shuddered like windblown flags, their structures tottering and their edges crumbling and shattering, undermining him and reshaping him. The clock on the wall was lost to his eyes. The passage of time was no longer a factor in the battle.

As the pressure upon him grew, so did his own desperation, so did his own reason, and so did his need for faith in himself and in the silhouette of his Soul.

"Help me," said Camlak to the moth-shadow.

"Help yourself," said the Soul, coaxing him, asking him for an effort.

"Heal me," pleaded Camlak, who felt himself torn across.

"Heal yourself," demanded the Soul.

Camlak's mind made hands in nowhere, and extended them outwards from the thin film of glistering light which spread him over the surface of sucking death. The hands reached into the naked, cold sky beyond his brain. They were reaching into *space*—a space he had never found before and known only by implication. It was real space, with volume and containment, but it was enfolded inside him, inside his body and his being. He was wrapped around a whole cosmos.

Soul space.

He formed hands and his hands formed claws, and the claws formed clutches and they reached up and up, and every shattering, shimmering, thread-held fragment of him cried:

"Help me!"

And the Soul said: "Help yourself."

The hands continued to ascend into the empty, wasted, derelict sky, feeling the cold and the needles of icelike fire beating into their palms, fraying and cracking the fingers and the claws.

Blood spilled.

But the hands did not matter.

The false flesh peeled off the unreal bones and the whited wreckage of the fingers still reached out into the sky, hauling at false arms and clutching with the *rigor* of death at the boundaries of the invaginated universe.

The thin strand of slime burst as the false shoulders erupted, and then, with a single convulsive movement, the *real* being grew, through the wall between the spaces, through the shattered puppet self, free from its existential womb.

Camlak opened his mouth to drag in air, gulping and swallowing and sucking. In the cage, the air flooded into the lungs. In the soul-space the ultimate coldness chilled the nascent self.

The head opened its eyes and felt them burn in the brightness, while the other felt pain and shock.

In the instant, Camlak was suspended, in transit, caught in the process of metamorphosis, turning himself outside-in like a snake swallowing its tail.

The mouth screamed: "Help me!"

And shadows clustered about the eyes, and claws reached out to grip his dead hands and his shoulders. Fingers twined in his hair and a million moth-shapes fluttered round and round his face in black cascades, casting a kaleidoscopic chaos of shadows on the darkening face of the carpet-mist which had been eating Camlak's mind.

Camlak was free.

Reborn, by the power of his will and his need. He burst into nowhere and he screamed in exultation.

35.

As Joth reached out to unfasten the door to Camlak's cage he saw the torpid rat's eyes whip open. Inside the eyes he watched a sudden flare of light.

Then Camlak's scream struck him down.

Iorga, behind him, suddenly lost control of his body and collapsed to the floor like a puppet with snapped strings.

Julea folded up without a sound.

Vicente Soron, who was coming through the door, pitched forward, the momentum of his movement throwing him against the banister of the cellar steps. The gun which he had found flew from his hand, released by limp fingers, and clattered on the tiled floor of the room.

Only Harkanter had been standing quite still at the instant of the scream. He, too, felt his mind suddenly disconnected from his body, imploded into utter blackness. But he was balanced, and he did not immediately fall. His body stood, held erect and still by muscles that were momentarily frozen.

Moments later, the muscles relaxed of their own accord, and Harkanter swayed, then rolled over with exaggerated slowness to meet the ground with a solid thump.

Joth's eyes did not close immediately. He fell, but he could still see what happened while he fell. He was the only one staring full at the prisoner at the instant of the scream.

He alone saw the instant of Camlak's disappearance.

The shape of the rat seemed to become completely fluid. The body flowed into a hole that opened a core of cold light somewhere within the space that the body had occupied. Very quickly, but in finite, measurable time, Camlak's body was collected into that hold and delivered *through* it.

The release which Joth had brought came an instant too late.

36.

The velocity of the shock wave was rather less than the speed of light. No electromagnetic radiation or sonic vibration was involved. The most sensitive instrumentation in the cybernet recorded only secondary phenomena—secondary, that is, relative to the Earthly continuum. Relative to the other space the wave itself was only an echo.

But it was an echo that woke a response.

The intensity of the reaction obeyed the inverse square law. Everyone within a mile or so of the location of the scream was affected in much the same way as those actually in the cellar. The reaction to the wave was the decoupling of all motor responses in the body—the effective isolation of the brain. The mechanism which permits such decoupling is located in the body known as the pons situated beneath the hind brain, and it may be assumed that it was within this body that the signal was received. Many of those affected within this range blacked out completely, and thus experienced nothing in the aftermath of the response. In other cases, however, the brain continued to operate although notionally cut off from all sensory input. The people so affected "dreamed," but the content of the dreams was only partly the issue of their own (subconscious) minds. A complex series of images transmitted by the modification of the shock wave itself were recorded, transcribed and reechoed within the program store of the subconscious mind. Engrammatic patterns were disturbed, destroyed and created. Almost all were to prove inviable, in the long term, and were broken up and erased by the mind's own defensive systems and faculties of self-repair. But that process would take time. In the meantime, the whole process of subconscious activity within the brain was disturbed. In no case was the disturbance so great as to cause permanent insanity.

Outside the critical radius at which the decoupling reaction was triggered there was no less of consciousness. By the same token, however, there was no immunity to the inflow of images. The extent to which the induced "dreams" interfered with the normal processes of brain activity varied according to the sensitivity of the individual, the type of activity ongoing in the particular brain at that moment, and—of course—the intensity of the stimulus as defined by the inverse-square law. The experiential blackout which defended many minds within the critical zone operated in a very few cases outside that zone, the strength of the signal being insufficiently strong, in most cases, to activate such a response even where available. Even so, a rather large number of individuals remained unaware that their brains had, in fact, been affected by the wave. Until these people began, in the near future, to suffer from "bad dreams" there would be no manifestation of the consequences of the event available to the conscious memory. Outside a radius of approximately twelve hundred miles, virtually all affected people fell into this category.

37.

Clea Aron, who was preparing for sleep, lying still in the darkness, allowing her thoughts to wander, actually felt the invasion of her mind like the blow of a fist to the back of her head. As the blow rocked her the blaze of confused images flooded her senses, causing her to gasp with pain.

She sat up and clutched her head in both hands. Following the initial shock there was a period of recoil, and then the images flooded her senses for a second time, more slowly, expanding and fragmenting. The experience was still too fast, and too complex, for her to sort out the imprints which were being stamped on the molecules which programmed her being, but she felt a few moments of utter strangeness that were beyond understanding. During those few moments she lived as an alien being with a wholly new identity.

She burst into tears and cried out aloud for someone to help her. Her own self reasserted itself, quickly and strongly, but the effects of the shock were absorbed.

That night, and every other night for many months, she would dream, and the dreams would belong only partly to herself.

38.

Enzo Ulicon was sitting in a chair examining printout from the supply unit at his deck when the wave hit. He felt it as a stabbing sensation at the base of his skull. His hands shook, briefly but violently, and the thin paper of the printout crumpled and ripped.

His eyes closed, reflexively, isolating him with the pain, so that he could concentrate his control. A series of patterns blossomed on the closed eyelids, and rushed back into his mind. The patterns swirled into pictures and for several minutes he became delirious, hurtled through a sequence of visionary instants which flared and were gone. It was barely possible to extract any sense from the flickering confusion, but Ulicon was calm and undisturbed. He identified the sensation, initially, as an ordinary headache—it did not occur to him that it was anything unfamiliar. He saw, therefore—and *knew* that he saw—the burning town, the firelit masks, the long, straight, corpse-littered road through the dark wilderness. He saw the fire-illumined cat face, and the multimillion-colored cankers, sills, dendrites, drapes and frills that comprised the life-system of the Swithering Waste. There was no sense in the sequence—no causality, no logic. It was simply an imaginative mosaic.

But Ulicon knew that he had looked into Hell.

He felt very frightened for a few moments, afterwards. But it was gone, and—so far as he knew—finished. The fear drained away. His hands were still unsteady, but they trembled very slightly, and he found that he could make them still by an effort of will.

Later in the night, he attempted to recall some of the images, reaching back into his memory. They rushed at him from the caverns of his mind, and once again he became the focus of the display. It was then that he realized that it was not finished, and perhaps never would be. Hell had been revealed, and he could not unlearn the revelation.

He, of all people, should have been able to cope with this discovery. It was he that had insisted so strongly that Rafael Heres and the others should become aware that there were two worlds of Earth, and not one.

Nevertheless, he doubted his sanity and he was suddenly possessed with the curious feeling that the floor beneath his feet was not secure, that at any moment it might begin to fracture, and precipitate him down, into darkness....

39.

Eliot Rypeck was already asleep, already dreaming. He was quiescent, save for his eyes, which moved beneath closed lids while his mind ran through its sequence of programs, its patterns of life, rehearsing them subconsciously and modifying them slightly by correlation with lately gained experience.

When the wave came he felt neither shock nor pain, but the mechanical process which occupied his brain was completely disrupted. The dream which was playing through his gray cells was shattered, the cytoarchitectural limitation of the process was lost, the neuronal messages were scrambled. He was ripped back into wakefulness by a sensory hurricane.

Within his dream, Rypeck howled in anguish. There was a momentary sensation of flight which quickly became one of falling, falling into a black vortex while the whirling world closed in and reached out a multitude of claws. As consciousness returned to flush out the aborted program, wipe the circuits clean, sweat stood out on his face and he felt the compulsion to *move*. He sat up in bed, as if jerked erect by strings.

He rocked slowly back and forth as he felt the whole garbled mess ebbing from his mind. He felt his body coming back to him, his sense of being swelling like a balloon to occupy every inch of his living frame.

The realization came to him that he had had a nightmare. That realization was infinitely more frightful than the thing itself. The connective routes in his thought processes were already well established. Nightmare...i-minus...Carl Magner.

The moment had come.

For a few seconds, the images returned, dancing at the threshold of consciousness. They flew all around him like fluttering moths, striking at his eyes from within.

Ulicon was right, he said, silently, chasing away the fugitive ideas with cold, vocalized thought. They came from outside. They came from outside into his mind.

One word swelled to the forefront of his mind, and would not die, dragging itself out and finally yielding only to an endless chain of echoes.

...invasion....

He lay back, and tried to force sleep to return. He was struck by the silly illusion that his whole awakening had been a fake, that he had merely reentered the macabre theater of his nightmare, enfolding himself within. But if this was a nightmare, it was real. He knew full well as he fought against wakefulness that he was not asleep, not dreaming, not hallucinating.

He was covered with sweat, and the sheets felt unbearably, glutinously warm against his body. After a few minues, he sat up again and mopped his face. He sat still, staring out into the darkness, at the thin sliver of the night sky which filtered in through the screened window. While he waited, his heartbeat began to settle.

But he could not get rid of the obsessive word which still ran faint echoes tumbling round the inside of his skull.

It turned out to be a very long night....

40.

The Ahrima were encamped to the south and west of Sagum, though parties of warriors covered north and east as well. The people of Sagum, forewarned by runners from Lehr, had elected to defend their town rather than desert it. They had stripped what they could from the fields, and strengthened the wall wherever significant improvement could be made in the time available. Even while the Ahrima rested before the assault the Children of the Voice worked ceaselessly, determined to hold the Ahrima and divert the horde if it were possible.

So far as they knew, no army was gathering in Shairn. The men of the towns were looking to their own and placing their faith in chance or destiny. The people of Sagum knew, however, that if they held the Ahrima for any length of time, warriors would come to them, in small groups, to harry the invaders from without, killing one or two at a time, destroying their supplies and poisoning their animals. If Sagum could hold, the Ahriman strength would be whittled away. The heartland of Shairn would grow relatively stronger. Stalhelm and Lehr had already taken some toll of the enemy's numbers.

On the other hand, if Sagum fell, the Ahrima would stay there, growing strong again on the produce of Shairan land, until they broke out to go whichever way they cared, with no town that would dare to stand against them. They would ravage the heartland and destroy the nation.

The fate of Sagum, therefore, seemed likely to determine the fate of Shairn.

Until the wave came.

The visions struck at the Ahrima, in sleep and in wakefulness. They saw what happened not as individual experience, but as collective experience. Every man knew that the visitation had come to all men, because not one warrior of the Ahrima was alone when the visions came.

There was not one among the Ahrima who could make sense of the "package" of images. To them, it was simply something that struck at the core of their being, something hostile and alien. It panicked them.

They turned away from Sagum, south to burned Lehr, and further south still, passing beyond the boundaries of Shairn into the lands of the Cuchumanate migration paths, and the isolated strongholds of the Men Without Souls.

Within the walls, however, the reaction was very different. The wave was no less a revelation to the Children of the Voice than to the Ahrima, but to them it was a revelation of an entirely different kind. They *could* see the images for what they were: the tangled memory web of one of their own kind. And more than that, they knew what had happened.

They knew it inside themselves, because they too had Gray Souls. When the impact of the wave turned their consciousness in upon itself, they did not find themselves isolated with confusion and fear. The Gray Souls were there. Even the Warriors and the little children achieved communion of a sort, without the aid of music or trance or the mind-smoothing juice of the weepweed. Those who knew how to use the communion, who already had the most effective rapport with the symbiotic Souls, discovered the whole truth. They learned that Camlak had broken the barrier, had everted himself into Soul space.

It was a miracle. Of course it was a miracle. Shairn was saved from the Ahrima, Camlak was free from a cage in Heaven, and a wave of force was traveling across and through the world and out into space announcing that Camlak and the Souls, together, had transcended the tyranny of space.

For the Children of the Voice, it was the advance warning of a new threshold in evolution, which was there to be crossed.

The realms of Tartarus were no longer imprisoned by the rotten Earth and the sky of steel.

41.

Rafael Heres was duelling with his doubts. He was alone, his mind was racing. He had advance warning of the various forces gathering about him. He knew that he had to face a revolt in his own ranks as well as the Eupsychian assault. He knew that the gloss had been taken off his Second Euchronian Plan in no uncertain terms by Harkanter's showmanship. He knew that he was deep in trouble, and that it might well take a miracle to save his political future.

The images came to him softly and quietly. There was no violence in the way they seeped into his mind. For a few moments, he lived within a mental environment where two realities conflicted for his attention. The safe, sane structures of his knowledge and his ego were forced to compete, for a few seconds, with the ghost of another being, the fragments of whose identity were strewn across the regions of Heres' inner world. It was neither startling nor particularly disturbing.

Merely strange. Only shadows, in his mind.

He was awake, rational and quick to realize that something had happened—something utterly new, for which he had no name and no explanation. He relaxed, and waited, observing himself closely to see if anything more was to come. Minutes passed, but he could find no further trace of strangeness.

He was prepared to forget the moment of weirdness. There seemed so little to it, and there was so much that he needed to think about.

Then the telephone began to ring. Urgently.

42.

Thorold Warnet experienced little more than a momentary tiredness and a slight sensation of dullness in the back of his head, which lasted less than a minute.

He set down his pen, and sat back in his chair, allowing himself to relax.

When he closed his eyes, pictures seemed to form in his mind, but they flitted so quickly through his thoughts that he could not focus on them. He was, however, moved to put his hand to his head and exert gentle pressure on his eyeballs with the thumb and forefinger.

It never occurred to him that anything dramatic had happened. But within minutes he, too, was called to his main deck and coopted into the worldwide scare.

43.

Sisyr was too far away for the wave to hit him with much force, but he picked it up faintly, and reacted immediately. He immediately sat up in bed and put his hands to his forehead, summoning his concentration as he came to his feet.

He was unable to recall the signal in detail, but when he exerted the full power of his faculties he was able to achieve playback of a kind. The images were blurred, and quite unidentifiable individually, but from the incomplete information he was able to gain a general impression of the sort of mind from which the message came, and the sort of sensory impressions which it contained.

He was, in any case, not really interested in the images carried by the wave—his principal concern was the fact that the wave had been broadcast at all.

He knew that this broadcast was intrinsically different from the kind of infiltration which had made Carl Magner's dreams into chaos. That, he felt sure, had been the leakage of images from a multitude of minds, which had at first irritated Magner's mind and gradually made it more and more sensitive as time went on. How Magner would have experienced the telepathic scream Sisyr did not know. Perhaps it would have destroyed his mind altogether.

The alien was certain that the wave had been generated by a single mind, amplified tremendously. How? Sisyr dismissed the idea that there had been supplementary augmentation. The sheer intensity of the experience which had torn the scream from the sender must have boosted the power of the broadcast.

Using the facilities of the cybernet it took Sisyr only a few moments to discover the focal point of the disturbance. The signal which he had picked up had traveled two thousand miles. He tried to estimate the power of the impulse at source, but could not make anything like an accurate guess. Obviously, however, the event which had been responsible for the generation of the wave was highly unusual.

Sisyr had not expected the manifestation to take this form. Nor had he expected it quite so soon, although the Magner phenomenon had been encouraging. He could not estimate the effect that the all-too-sudden revelation might have on the people of Earth. Not merely the Children of the Voice, but the humans. The people of the Overworld must have received a shock which could revise their whole attitude to life. No doubt they would get over the shock itself, but once the barrier was breached....

Once started, these processes did not stop.

Sisyr felt no excitement as he compiled the message which he would transmit to the stars. It was not a time for congratulations. Not yet. It was a delicate time, for close observation, for patience and for careful action.

The message which he transmitted would not reach the outpost for forty years or more. It would take even longer for the answer to come back—they would bring it in person.

The contents of the message were simple enough. It was simply to say that the gateway was there, and that it had opened for the first time.

He wasted no time in sending it, but there was no hurry. It was not an urgent message. Sisyr had all the time in the world. *This* world.

His world.

44.

Randal Harkanter was a strong man. He was a brave man and a determined one. But these are relative terms. Among the listless citizenry of the Overworld he was virtually a man alone, an altogether exceptional case. By other standards, perhaps he was only a man with some kind of drive.

Of those in the cellar, however, he was the first to begin to recover from the effects of the mental explosion. He regained consciousness before Joth, and before Iorga (who was, by any human standards, tough and strong). The distance between them may have played some part. Joth, a mere arm's length away from Camlak, had taken the full intensity. Iorga was a pace or two behind Joth. Harkanter had been hanging back, and to the side—perhaps twice as far away as the cat. While Harkanter was beginning to rediscover his arms and legs, the hellkin's brain and body were still at odds, the brain in turmoil and the motor nerves switched off.

Harkanter was quick to realize his advantage. He looked

both forward and back, and could see no sign of life anywhere. Apparently, neither Julea nor Soron was making any attempt to recover themselves, but Soron might have been knocked out when he fell on the steps.

The big man tried to raise his body, but the moment he lifted his head there was a wave of dizziness which threatened to black him out. Instead, he began to crawl, hauling himself slowly and painfully across the tiles. His arms and legs would not work as he commanded them, but he moved by virtue of a series of convulsive jerks. He found himself breathing very heavily, sweating cold, with faintness ebbing up within him every time he made any sort of real effort. His body did not want to obey his mind, and the instructions were somehow garbled in between thought and action, but he moved, gradually.

He moved toward the gun which had flown from Vicente Soron's hand to land on the floor of the cellar.

It was a small handgun, but it was a genuine weapon, not the anesthetic dart-gun which the naturalist had carried in the Underworld. It was not one of Harkanter's guns—Soron had apparently been sufficiently frightened by his experiences in the Underworld to obtain one of his own.

Harkanter was actually reaching for the gun when the backlash came. His mind had absorbed the energy of the discharge completely—Harkanter was not aware that his brain had been working during the period of unconsciousness. So far as he was concerned, it was completely black time. But now, as the normal patterns of thought and the cohesiveness of self began to reassert themselves, the way was clear for the images to display themselves. The energy which had flooded into the mind now flooded out again, as though a coiled spring were released.

From Harkanter's point of view, it was sheer insanity. His hand was snatched back from the gun before his fingers touched the butt, and he writhed like a wounded worm. The images flashed inside his brain like a firework display. Real pain racked his body.

It lasted only a few seconds, but it reduced him once again

to near helplessness. He failed to collect himself; his muscles worked of their own accord. His fingers clenched and unclenched with such fierceness that his fingernails tore into his palms. He soiled himself.

In the meantime, Iorga became conscious. He watched Harkanter's agonies for a time, quite dispassionately. But then he saw the big man begin to reassert his will, and he saw the gun on the floor. He realized what was happening. He too began to reach for his weapon.

It was a strange and desperate race. Subjectively speaking, it was also a long race, although by the hands on the clock it took place within the span of a few seconds. The complexity of the actions involved made it a long race, in terms of mental coordination and control. Harkanter had to reach the handgun, take it into his fist, steady himself enough to aim it, get his fore-finger round the trigger and...if necessary, or desirable...fire it. Iorga already had the gun which Joth had asked him to carry—the rifle. It was underneath his fallen body. But he, too, had a struggle before him. He had to lift himself, roll clear of the gun, grip the weapon, and then lift it into position. Then...it depended on Harkanter. Iorga had no intention of firing unless fired at.

Beyond the moment of firing—or not firing, as the case might be—neither man had any thought. They were both concen-trating on the immediate task. Had they stopped to think about the future, they would have condemned themselves to failure in the present. To do what they were trying to do they needed all their strength and complete commitment.

Harkanter's groping fingers finally touched the pistol.

Iorga found his body moving, found himself coming clear of the rifle. But the mechanism of the gun caught in his clothing, and the gun began to drag along the floor with him as he moved.

Harkanter pecked at the gun with fingers that would no longer close. Blood running from his palms dripped on to the tiles. The gun rocked on its chamber, and the butt spun away from him.

Joth was beginning the long journey back from oblivion.

Iorga planted both hands on the rifle, one on the stock and

the other half way along the barrel. He grappled it free of the entanglement. He lost balance and rolled backwards, but the gun was free. He was laid out flat on one side, the barrel was pointed the wrong way. He began to turn it, trying to bring it to bear on the crawling Harkanter before trying to come to grips with the trigger mechanism.

Harkanter dabbed at the pistol, uselessly.

Time dragged by, and nothing happened. Vicente Soron sat up on the staircase and looked through the guardrail, trying to understand what was happening.

Joth opened his eyes.

Julea, now conscious, kept hers closed tight. She did not want to know. She hardly knew whether she wanted to be alive.

Harkanter got his hand round the butt of the gun and picked it up. He rocked back on to his haunches and tried with his other hand to force his finger round the trigger.

Somehow, his groping released the safety catch. He heard it click and knew that all he had to do was press. A burst of elation helped sensibility to return. He got his finger inside the trigger guard.

Iorga was picking up the rifle. It seemed incredibly heavy and cumbersome. He heaved at it, almost like a weightlifter trying to press a dumbbell. He heaved again, at himself rather than the apparent dead weight of the gun. His body was working again, the gun came up, and slotted naturally into his grip.

Joth tried desperately to clear his head, and in trying to speak he managed a groan.

Julea heard the groan.

Soron remembered something, and tried to shout, but no sound came.

Harkanter leveled the pistol and fired.

Iorga watched the dark finger tighten on the trigger. He reacted immediately, without conscious decision. Sheer inertia carried him through to the endpoint of his action, just as it carried Harkanter through to the endpoint of his.

The hammer of the pistol clicked harmlessly. The chamber

was empty.

Iorga had already returned the fire. There was no way to hold the action.

The rifle bullet blew Harkanter's head off.

45.

All over the continent, the holovisual network was carrying an interview which featured Abram Ravelvent and Vicente Soron. Other time zones were scheduled to see the recording at the same relative time, as they moved into night. They never actually got to see it at all.

While Soron, in the flesh, was trying to drag himself back through the cellar door, desperate to escape from the threat of Iorga's gun (an imaginary threat, as the recoil had thrown the hellkin back, and ripped the rifle from his hands) his image was in closeup in a million homes, ten times life-size, telling the world what the Underworld was like.

The world was not listening. It had other things on its mind. But the broadcast continued.

There was a certain irony in its contents.

After Soron had finished, Yvon Emerich turned to Ravelvent and said: "What do you think of the idea that the rats might be the dominant species in the Underworld?"

"I think it's absurd," said Ravelvent.

"But the evidence...."

"...is virtually worthless. We have, apparently, one specimen. I haven't seen it, but I can't doubt Vicente's word that it is what he claims. Once having accepted that, however, it is by no means logical that one should proceed to say that the Underworld is full of beings like this. We still know virtually nothing. We can make no reasonable guess at all as to what might be the dominant species in the Underworld. We have no justification, in fact, for thinking in terms of 'Dominant species' at all."

"But suppose," said Emerich, "that it was confirmed that the rats *are* the dominant species down there. What then?"

"I refuse to suppose any such thing," said Ravelvent stubbornly.

"You are a scientist," said Emerich. "Very well, let us adopt as a scientific *hypothesis* the assumption that the Underworld is primarily inhabited by creatures of the rather fearsome type which Vicente has described...."

"Fearsome?" queried Ravelvent, determined to stop Emerich from loading his questions, if possible.

"It is fearsome," said Emerich, definitely. "I can assure you of that. In the photographs we have, it is quiescent, but let us look at the figures. It is rather more than four feet long—or perhaps I should say four feet *high*, as it walks on two feet rather than four. It has hands and a considerable cranial cavity, big enough—Vicente suggests—to hold a brain of near-human complexity and capability. And we *do* have, here, the knife with which it was threatening to murder Randal Harkanter when Vicente shot it with an anesthetic dart."

Emerich pressed the knife into Ravelvent's hand, making him inspect it in front of the cameras.

"You'll notice," intervened Soron, "that it testifies to a far higher degree of tehnology extant in the Underworld than any of us could have dared to suggest might exist down there. Are we to believe that this weapon came into the hands of the rat from somewhere else, or is it remotely possible that there exists in the world below a society of rats which is advanced enough to pose a definite threat to human life?"

Ravelvent was temporarily defeated by the way that Soron had phrased his question, which suggested all kinds of horrific but tentative possibilities.

"I don't know how the rat got his hands on the knife," said Ravelvent, "but he didn't make it. I don't believe this was made in the Underworld at all. I think it was made up here."

"Are you suggesting...?" Soron began.

"No," said Ravelvent, quickly, "I'm not suggesting that you planted it, or that any member of your expedition took it down there. I'm suggesting that there has, for many centuries—probably dating back to the early days of the Plan—been clandestine dealing between the Overworld and the surface. I don't know who is involved or why, but I do know that it happens. If you trace the flow of materials as recorded in the cybernet you'll find that there has been a steady drain. The missing materials must go to the Underworld because there is nowhere else for them to go. *That's* what your knife proves. It says nothing at all about the possibilities of rat civilizations. *Nothing.*"

Ravelvent settled back in his chair, satisfied that he had turned the entire course of the argument with his revelation. He believed that he had stamped hard on Emerich's scare story. Emerich, however, was not a man to give up easily.

"The rat had the knife," he said, "and was prepared to use it. Whether the object itself came from the Overworld or not does not alter the fact that the rat was possessed of it. If there has, as you say, been a steady supply of materials to the Underworld—a fact of which I was aware, but hesitant to confirm—there can be no doubt that some of these materials are adopted and used by the rats. Does that not suggest that the rats have evolved to the point at which they pose a danger to human beings?"

"We can't assume any such thing," said Ravelvent.

"But we cannot neglect the possibility?" persisted Emerich.

There was no answer.

"In that case," said Emerich, "isn't the idea of opening the Underworld—*for any purpose whatsoever*—a very dangerous one indeed?"

Ravelvent opened his mouth to reply.

When the recording had been made, Ravelvent *had* replied, but at this point the tape was cut short.

Yvon Emerich appeared, in different clothes, broadcasting live. He explained the program had been cut off because of the strange and terrible event which had swept the world while it was in progress. He assured the people that every effort was being made to find out what had happened and why.

As soon as it was possible, Emerich assured the world, the

explanation would be discovered and a full account of the happening released. In the meantime, live broadcasting would continue, as the anatomy of the phenomenon was explored, and as information came in.

Emerich himself would not be fronting the broadcast—he wanted to be behind the scenes, sifting the information and deciding how and when it was to be released. Before he handed over to someone else he announced that no deaths or serious injuries had—as yet—been recorded as a result of the phenomenon.

46.

"You were warned," said Ulicon.

"I was warned," Heres admitted. "Never mind that now. There's no time for an orgy of recrimination. You told me it wasn't finished but I tried to bury it anyway. Eliot's been trying to stab me in the back ever since. Now it's blown up. You can go ahead with the back-stabbing if you think that's what's called for. But this is serious. It's no time for petty quarreling."

"I accept that," said Ulicon.

"All right. Now—you were the one who warned us all that the Magner affair might blow up. Give me an explanation of what happened tonight."

"An explanation! How can I? Rafe, I don't *know* what happened. What you describe as having happened to you is *not* what happened to me. You experienced something utterly strange.... I had visions that were starkly clear and quite terrifying. Right now the holo is throwing out all sorts of garbage—people knocked unconscious, mental explosions.... There's no way of knowing whether there was one event or half a million. How can I possibly give you an explanation until we have some clear idea of how the thing maps out?"

"We can't wait," said Heres. "When we discussed the Magner affair in Close Council, you were the only one ready with some guesses. You were the one with ideas. We need those ideas now. Why do you think I called you? This is a sealed circuit, Enzo, and half the world is at my back. I've got to find answers of some kind. Give me something to play with, please! Because if I can't quell this panic, Heaven only knows where we'll be come the morning."

"All right," said Ulicon, trying to halt Heres' flow of words with a gesture. "I'll tell you what I think. But this is sheer fantasy. It could be nothing like the truth.

"When I investigated Magner I made the point that the visions only came to him during sleep, but that they weren't ordinary dreams. I guessed that there was some kind of telepathic link tied in with the sleep process, possibly involving the pons. I guessed that Magner was picking up some kind of leakage from minds in the Underworld. I stand by those guesses.

"What happened tonight was related, but by no means similar. The visions came to *me* while I was awake. They not only came, but they stayed. They've come into my head and they've *stuck*. That isn't leakage—this...message...has been driven into my mind with real power behind it. And into yours, and—so far as we know—into every other human mind on the planet. To some, the message was meaningless, to others the impact of receiving it was like a physical blow—just as bright light or loud noise can *hurt* physically.

"First point of advice—find someone who got the *whole* message and got it clear. What I got was a mess of fragments. Maybe that's what was sent out, but we can't afford to overlook the possibility that someone is walking around with a complete understanding of what's going on because he got the content of the broadcast loud and clear. Maybe the word *message* is all wrong, and what hit us wasn't a deliberate attempt to communicate. If that's the case, we have a real problem, because like it or not we have communication. Mind to mind. Imagination to imagination. Whether the human race likes it or not, it has just been awarded telepathy. We might not be able to transmit to one another, or to read one another's minds, but *our minds can be invaded* from without. That's the crucial fact.

"At the very least, we need a method of defense. We need to be able to screen out anything like this that happens in the future. Because it is *going* to happen in the future. Magner showed us the writing on the wall and we let it go. Now it's here. Tomorrow morning, or tomorrow night, it can happen again. It will—if not tomorrow then the day after, or the day after that. This *could* be the beginning of the greatest thing that ever happened to us—but unless we can understand and control it, then it could be one of the worst

"Find out what happened, at all costs. Find some singular event at the focal point of this phenomenon which we can correlate with the mental transmission. Find out the entire contents of the transmission. Find out who, or what, sent that message. Find out how, but above all else find out *why*. Until you know that there's no way you can promise the people that it isn't going to happen again every day from now until doomsday. Perhaps you'll never be able to make that promise, because perhaps it *will* happen again, and again, every night from now until doomsday."

"What did you see?" demanded Heres, after a momentary pause. "Exactly."

"It wasn't exact," said Ulicon. "I don't know even a fraction of what I saw. I don't want to know. All I can give you are the pieces of the jigsaw. I saw the Underworld. I'm sure of that. Not one part of it but many. Not a panoramic view from above but a vast series of images, like still photographs, of many different places. I saw...creatures...people...things. I saw faces that were covered in fur, but not beast faces. I wish I'd seen that rat of Harkanter's, because it might allow me to be more sure. I saw many things which were like animals, but also like men. I saw one, in particular, that was not like the others—but it, too, was part-animal, part-man. I saw real men, I think, but their images were confused with painted masks. They seemed too large and utterly savage. The whole thing was somehow out of focus. Not blurred, but *wrong*. There wasn't much color, because all the images were dim, but the colors that there were seemed out of balance. All the signals were mixed—it was like looking at an optical illusion...one of those drawings which show impossible things, like staircases going round in a circle, upwards all the way. There was nothing like that in the images, but they gave the same sense of wrongness...wrongness that I couldn't pin down. It might be the effect of—as it were—seeing with someone else's eyes, experiencing the world *via* a different balance of sensory information. It might well be...but I don't know. I can't be sure. I don't know what I was seeing, but I'll tell you this... it was a vision of Hell...the Hell that Magner put into his book. I can imagine now what that man went through. I understand what he wrote. But if that was a cry for help, then it was the fiercest and most frightening cry imaginable. I don't believe it was, I think it was Magner who made it into one. That was his interpretation—his way of making sense of it all."

"And your way?" prompted Heres. "How do you make sense of it all?"

"I can't," said Ulicon. "Perhaps I never shall. All I'm sure of is the central fact. My mind has been invaded. Someone or something down there in the Underworld can make me hear him inside my head, see as he sees."

"Suppose," said Heres, "that he can hear you. See as you see."

"How would I know?" replied Ulicon. "How could I ever know?"

"Enzo," said Heres, suddenly becoming the Hegemon again. "I want you to take charge of things within the Movement. Recruit what help you need. The first thing to do is to keep the Councillors calm and silent. I'll put Luel on to handling Emerich and his crew. Get busy, and get as many people as possible busy. Make out that the entire Movement is a hive of activity, and for Heaven's sake try to preserve an illusion of competence. Whether we know what we're doing or not let's pretend that we have it all under control. Never mind the public—make sure the Council and the Movement believe it. Delegate whatever authority you can. Put everybody in charge of something, even if it's only putting other people in charge of other things. Create some work, and make sure it's hard work. Get the real schedule under way, but don't leave anyone idle, whether they have anything to contribute or not. All right?"

"I'm with you," said Ulicon.

The link was broken.

Ulicon wondered whether he had done the right thing. Maybe he was a fool to stay with Heres. Maybe Heres would steer the Movement straight into the heart of the trouble. He had been wrong once. Perhaps twice. But in this extreme situation, one had to have stability of command...someone had to hold things together...there had to be someone who could take the load of responsibility...off one's own back.

Mechanically, Ulicon began obeying his orders.

Meanwhile, Heres was sitting alone with just one thought.

We have been *invaded.*

47.

Alwyn Ballow was at the very heart of the massive operation to find out what had happened, how, and why. He was surrounded by screens and lineprinters, keyboards and microphones. Information flowed around him in a never-ceasing stream. He was in the seat of judgment, sorting out the flow, picking from it the significant morsels, allowing the rest to disappear into mute electronic storage. He was the brain coordinating the central nervous system of the cybernet. He was God monitoring the puppet strings on which the human race was dancing. (Or, from an alternative viewpoint, he was the maggot at the very core of Euchronian's apple.)

Yvon Emerich was at a much smaller deck, behind Ballow. He too was the brain, or God (or the maggot). That which Ballow sorted out was fed through to Emerich. Emerich collated it, reorganized it, shaped it for release. Ballow judged, Emerich commanded. Between them, they controlled Euchronia's knowledge and—far more important—Euchronia's belief. While Heres was forming the broadcast of Camlak's scream into an invasion, Emerich and Ballow were making it into a spectacle.

"Crash on seven," Ballow recited. "Car spun off highway. No injuries."

Screen seven continued to testify with regard to the accident, but neither Ballow nor Emerich gave it any further attention.

"On nine," chanted Ballow. "Car ran on uncontrolled... police...here's something...! En route for Harkanter's address... get this! Harkanter's house is in the middle of the black area... whatever happened is inside there. Find out who made that call! Call Harkanter! Get an eye over Harkanter's place immediately...track any vehicles, including that police car...."

"What's that on five?" (Emerich)

"Crash...coming in now...two dead.... Makes five so far, Yvon. Safeties failed, manual interference...third time that's happened...can't have been a clean knockout.... Hold on for the printer...reports from fringes of the dead spot. Here's one claims he saw a massacre...a burning town...we already have that...check against Magner's stuff.... More people claiming they saw people in the Underworld.... Reports of recurrence by the score...medical still blank...."

"Forget all the what-I-saw business. It's getting us nowhere. Those medic teams *must* be in the no-answer area by now."

"One of the car crashes caused a minor blackout...some faculties out of op...fail-safes in, no communication...east side of black area. Other homes should be unaffected.... Police have reached Harkanter's place...report says call made by Vicente Soron—illicit invasion of privacy—no details...says Soron was in a flat panic...hey!...eye nine has something. Check nine. Close up...give us more detail nine...."

"Hell, it's only a car!"

"It's going the *wrong* way. It's come *out* of the dead area... sure it's had time to cross it...plenty of time...but we didn't spot it going in...get closer...no, I know you can't show me who's driving...find out who owns...oh, it's public...okay, keep on it.... Keep calling Harkanter...the police are there now...they'll answer as soon as it suits them...just keep running the bell....

"...Yvon, there's a suicide here...ties in. They have a note but they say it makes no sense...put it on the screen...makes no sense to me.... I can't quite make out the writing...man's name Simkin Cinner...something about ghosts and revenge...must have taken the visions pretty hard....

"...we have a trace of the log of that car coming out of the dead area...it's public, its journey was tracked automatically... it was driven out earlier...is that Harkanter's house? Check with the map.... Yvon, that car is coming from Harkanter's house... must be connected with the i.o.p. call...."

"Stop the car!"

"Can't...don't have authority to override...."

"Get it."

"We're trying...take time, though...."

"Hell, it'll take an age to work through the police hierarchy... they'll get to where they're going long before. Keep that eye in close. Any chance of getting a vehicle to intercept?"

"The police have what we have, Yvon...if they won't override they won't intercept...they have their own chain of command tangled...something's wrong here, Yvon. They shouldn't be fouled up this way."

"Policemen have brains too," Emerich pointed out. "They got this thing between the eyes just the same as we did. Maybe worse. We got off light, to judge by some of these scare stories."

"...they've completed the scan of the area...no further crashes. Death toll stands at five, probably five only...six including the suicide...maybe more inside the houses...accidents, maybe shock...call to Harkanter's place is through...."

"I'll take it," snapped Emerich, and moved forward to the switches on his own phone. Ballow's attention was momentarily diverted to the printout, and when he turned again to Emerich the news had already broken.

"Alwyn! Get Soron. In here. I don't care how, but move

Heaven and Earth if you have to. Get Soron here."

"What happened?"

"Harkanter's been killed. Soron saw the whole thing. If the police want to keep him get someone in with him. Get a link of some kind—I want to talk to him as soon as humanly possible...."

Emerich's attention returned to the screen. Someone was still trying to tell him something.

"Gone?" he said. "Gone where?"

Ballow sent a quick stream of instructions into one of the microphones.allow sent a quick stream of instructions into one of the microphones.

"Get a scan from one of the eyes," said Emerich. "Low down, round Harkanter's house. High resolution. The rat's loose. You probably won't pick it up, but try."

"...Heres continues unavailable," reported Ballow. "Who else can we try? They don't think Heres will say anything at all. Not tonight...."

"Get that woman," said Emerich. "The one they put on in the Magner debate. *Her* thoughts ought to be worth a penny or two right now. Clea Aron...get her. And get that friend of Magner's... the one who was with him when he was shot. Abram Ravelvent. I was talking to him on screen last night—it was his recording that we had to chop. He's full of ideas about the Underworld— find out what *he* has to say about this...."

"...More in on Harkanter," said Ballow. "He was shot dead. Nothing more. They won't let us near Soron...not the police— the Movement...they've claimed him...Yvon! They're trying to close us down!"

"Have you got Aron?"

"She's not available."

"Ravelvent?"

"Just left home.... That car! It's stopped...get that eye in closer...that building is the plexus where Harkanter's expedition went down to the Underworld. It's where the door is.... I can't see them clearly in this light. Two, maybe three...they must be going down...you think the rat might be with them?"

Emerich was staring at his screen again.

"You can't close down," he was saying. "You can't just black out the holovisuals all over the world."

Ballow switched into the call. The man at the other end was Luel Dascon—Rafael Heres' chief satellite.

"We have the authority," said Dascon. "A state of emergency was declared a few moments ago. We are taking over all media. We will continue to broadcast, but your people may not interfere in any way whatsoever."

"You can't do that!" said Emerich, loudly.

"Please hand over all facilities to the authorized representatives of the Council," said Dascon smoothly. "They should be with you now."

"They are," put in Ballow.

"I'm telling you," said Emerich, his face white with anger, "that if Heres has any ideas of winning the petitioned election he can forget them! I'll kill his chances stone dead for this."

"There isn't going to be an election," said Dascon. "The state of emergency overrules the petition. We're all in this together, Yvon. All the quarreling is over. We have to unite now...against a common enemy."

48.

When Ravelvent arrived at the plexus, Julea was still in the car. The camera eye was hovering in the sky, shining with the reflection of the silver dawn light, but with that exception she was alone. The car's microphone was still in her hand. She was not crying, but her face was flushed and the look in her eyes suggested that she simply could not find the tears.

"What happened?" said Ravelvent.

It was the wrong question. She gave him a look that was angry, almost hateful. He led the car door open while he took her arm and guided her gently out on to the verge at the side of the road. Her eyes were drawn to the door to the mechanical nerve complex—the door which gave access to a staircase into the world below. It stood ajar. They had stood here before, the two of them, not daring to pass beyond the doorway themselves. They had waited, and nothing had happened.

"He's not coming back," said Ravelvent, gently. He meant her father, Carl Magner.

"He is," she said. "He said so. He said that he would come back, but he had to go." She was not talking about her father but about Joth.

"It's all right now," said Ravelvent. "It's all over."

"No," she said. "It won't ever be over. He killed him. That won't ever end."

Ravelvent looked around for something to put over her shoulders, because she was obviously cold. But there was nothing in either of the cars. He put his arms round her instead, and hugged her close.

"Let's go home," he said. "My home. Not your father's empty house. Come home with me. It'll be all right."

She shook her head, and squirmed out of his grasp. He withdrew his hands and stood still, feeling rather lonely.

"Joth's coming back," she said. "It's Joth who went down there. He brought me here. I couldn't drive back. I had to call you. But we must wait. For Joth."

Ravelvent was at a loss.

"Before you called," he said, half turning away so that he did not seem to be talking to her at all, "the strangest thing happened. I was doing some work...some programming, for the educational facilities...I was deliberately not watching the holovision, because I knew that I was on and I didn't want to see, when...it was like a bomb going off in my head...and now, I have the crazy feeling that I can see...visions...as your father saw them. I can see the Underworld, Julea. I *know* it was true. It's not a game any more."

"It's not a game," she said, soberly. "He's dead."

"Who?"

"Randal Harkanter."

"*Who?*"

"The Underworlder shot him. It was...like a bomb going off in his head...."

"What *happened*?" demanded Ravelvent, for the second time. He was facing her again now, and his voice was raised.

She wouldn't say anything. She wanted to cry but she couldn't. He tried to take hold of her again, but she stepped backwards.

"It's all right," he tried to insist. "Whatever it was, it's over now. It was only a bad dream. It's over now. You must come home with me. It'll be all right, there. It's *over* now."

"No," she replied. "Not now. It won't ever be over."

Then she let him lead her to his car, and drive her away. The other car, which Joth had requisitioned from the omni-benevolent machine which served all life in the Overworld, remained.

Waiting.

49.

"Eliot," said Heres, "I'm asking for your help. What happened yesterday and the day before simply doesn't matter now. We wake up this morning to a new world. We have to face that. There's no point in dragging all the old, tired arguments behind us now. Eleven thousand years of Euchronian history ended last night. This morning, the Millennium is meaningless. The argument about the relevance of the i-minus agent is shifted into an entirely new dimension. If you continue to push your petition for an election you could destroy the Movement. I'm asking you for your sake, and my sake, and for the sake of the whole world, to forget our differences and help me."

"Do I have a choice?" said Rypeck, bitterly.

"Would I be asking you if you hadn't?"

"The petition falls in any case. You're the Hegemon and you've taken a tight hold on your Hegemony. The disaster which you may have caused with your willful blindness has come, and you've taken advantage of it to confirm your power. You have a frightened world, Rafael, and they turn to you because you've forbidden them to turn anywhere else. You're riding high, Rafael. But where to? I've been trying to call you for hours and getting nothing but a blank wall. Now you call me, and you ask for my help. Why, Rafael? Are you sure, now, of everyone else? Everyone but the Eupsychians? Are you trying to close the ranks completely?"

"If that's the way you want to put it," said Heres, "that's what I'm trying to do. We can't afford to have the Council divided now. I need your loyalty and I'm asking for it. Euchronia faces danger and tragedy, and we need Euchronian unity—singleness of mind and singleness of purpose. We have been invaded, Eliot. The invasion has struck into our very minds. You were right when you said that we are ignorant. We are worse than ignorant—"we are vulnerable. We've all made mistakes—the whole Movement has left itself unready to cope with what struck at us last night. But now we have to cover for those mistakes. We have to unmake them. We have to deal with the threat which Euchronian society faces. If this thing gets loose, we will be destroyed. Now I ask you, Eliot, do you want to try to apportion blame—to waste your efforts in bitterness and recrimination— or do you want to help. Are you with me, or against me?"

And Rypeck realized, inevitably, that he didn't have a choice.

"Yes, Rafe," he said, "I'm with you. Let's save the world. How do you propose to go about it?"

50.

Joth half-expected that they would be waiting at the bottom of the stairway. He was ready, if it proved necessary, to fight his way back into the Underworld. And yet he did not intend to stay. He only wanted to tell Nita what had happened—to explain why he had not returned her father to his world.

But the scientists in the camp were far too preoccupied to be guarding the door with guns. They, too, had been invaded during the night, first torn from their sleep and then kept back from it by the nightmares which threatened to engulf them whenever their eyes closed and their mind relaxed from conscious ratiocination. They had assumed, in the beginning, that the experience was theirs alone: that the Underworld had reached out to punish them for *their* invasion, that the dreams came because they were strangers in an alien world. They came together, to talk, because they felt the need for company, and for some collaborative exercise to occupy their thoughts and senses. They were afraid—desperately afraid.

By the time that dawn broke in the world above, and Joth and Iorga returned to the world of the fixed stars, the expeditionary force had learned that what they had experienced had also swept the upper world like a great tidal wave. It had changed the current of their argument, in frantic search of an explanation, but it had not alleviated their fear or their need to huddle together, cowering from the perpetual night. The man with the metal face and the hellkin escaped into the Swithering Waste unnoticed.

There they met Chemec, who had waited patiently for their return for many hours whose passage he had no way to measure.

He, too, had dreamed. He, of all people, should have known what was happening, but in fact he, alone, remained completely unmoved and undisturbed by the images which had flooded his mind. He had not been aware that they came from elsewhere. The scenes that were plucked from Camlak's ego might just as well have come from his own. He believed that he had seen only things which came from within himself, woven into the distorted, tattered cloth of a commonplace nightmare. Such things did not worry Chemec, who was used to nightmares. Had he kept closer company, within himself, of his Gray Soul, perhaps he would have known that something new and strange had happened to him, but Chemec was not a man who made much use of his Soul.

Possession of a Soul is no guarantee of understanding.

But Chemec led Joth and Iorga back to one who did know, and who was even beginning to understand. Nita, like the cripple, might have confused Camlak's mindblast with something echoing out of the inwardness of her own being, but her mind was younger than Chemec's, and she slept much closer to her Soul. She had heard Camlak's scream of anguish and pain as he had torn himself free from external space, and she had sensed the ripple which had been created in the fabric of space by that tearing, and which had acted as a carrier wave for the image-charged emotion which had been generated within his mind by the scream.

She knew, therefore, some time before Joth came back, that Camlak was no longer in the Overworld—no longer in the world at all.

"I think your father destroyed himself," Joth told her.

She shook her head.

"He was in the cage, and then he was gone. Absolutely. The force hit us, took our bodies away from our minds, left us fallen and helpless. It wasn't the force of an explosion. It didn't hurt us, but Camlak just disappeared."

"We felt it too," said Huldi.

"Camlak didn't die," Nita explained. "He found something the priests have always told us about. No one ever found it before. The priests couldn't know. But they were right. It was there."

"What did he find?" asked Joth.

"A way between the worlds," she said. "Not your world and mine. Another world."

"Where?"

"Nowhere. Enclosed within us. Deep. We can look into it sometimes, at the Communion of Souls. You remember. You saw."

Joth stared at her, uncomprehending. He had seen the Communion of Souls. He had interpreted it, to his own satisfaction. And he had been right—he was sure of that. Now he realized that he had not been right enough. He had seen only the tiniest fraction of the reality. He wondered where he could find the help which he needed in order to begin to know the truth. Huldi knew nothing—hers was only an animal mind whose sentience served animal purposes. She never asked herself questions, let alone created answers. Iorga, too, had little or no use for words except as signals. If he used them within himself, to try to come to terms with the reality in which he was a prisoner, he showed no outward sign of it. Chemec might some day come to understand what Nita knew now, but it would mean nothing to him. His way of life was Yami's way—the way that answered all challenges with the will to kill. And the people of the Overworld...how could they ever *begin* to understand, while they had made of themselves what they were?

Joth abandoned the tangled web of thought, without surrendering to the insidious despair.

"What will you do now?" he asked Nita.

"I don't know," she said.

"Will you do something for me?" he asked.

"Yes."

"I'm going back, now. I want to put right all the lies and the mistakes. I don't know what will happen to me, but I don't think they'll blame me for what Iorga did. I want to find out all they know, and why they know so little when men like Burstone must know so much more. But there's something else I want to know—something else I think is important. I want to know why there is a road of stars which leads from the edge of the Waste into the black lands. A road must lead somewhere, and it's a road that was left for you to follow, not for me. I can track it, from above—I think. If not, I'll come back and follow you down here, if I can. Either way, I'll try to find you at the other end."

They did not ask him for a reason. They lived their lives, for the most part, without reasons. Because they lived almost without time, they did not need to make plans out of their lives. Only Chemec had enough fear of the black lands to refuse what Joth had asked.

Chemec did not go. He went, alone, back to the country called Shaira. Nita, Huldi and Iorga took the Road of Stars. They all loved one another.

Joth, whom they also loved, went home.

51.

The head of Rafael Heres hung like a bloated balloon in every home in Euchronia. Somewhere in the world it was midnight, somewhere else it was noon. It made no difference. The head was there, and the whole world was listening, watching the bloodless lips move. No one was missing out on sleep to listen. Wherever it was night, in Euchronia, it was a sleepless night.

"The purpose of the Euchronian Movement and the Euchronian Plan," Heres was saying, "was to build a world for men to live in peace. From the wreckage of a dying world the Euchronians made a new world grow. They designed that world for mankind, because they wanted their children—their ultimate children—to be able to live the kind of lives *they* wanted to live, but could not. They wanted to build a paradise for their children, and they did.

"We are those children. We live in the world that they made for us. We have used it as well as we could, and perhaps we have not used it as well as they would have wanted us to. But this is a new world, and there is time yet. There is time for us to become the children that the Euchronian Planners would have wished to inherit the new Earth.

"Our fathers wanted to give us a world which was not merely ideal for the purposes of mankind, but a world which was secure—whose own future was guaranteed. They designed our world to be stable—in a state of balance. They never claimed—they were never arrogant enough to claim—that ours would be a perfect world, but they wanted it to be a world where we could live our lives completely safe from the tragedies which they suffered as a matter of course. They wanted it to be a world where men could be free, and free forever.

"Our freedom is threatened now.

"Our stability is threatened now.

"Our world is threatened now.

"The Planners gave to us all that we have, to hold for all time. They never envisaged—they never could have envisaged—that a terrible threat to our way of life might emerge, not from within our society, nor from the infinite reaches of space in which our Earth is only a mote of dust, but from the old world—the world they interred as a failure, a disaster, and a ruin. The Euchronians left the past behind them, thinking that it was obliterated, cut off forever from the light of the sun and the face of Heaven. But that past has caught up with Euchronia.

"Our minds are no longer completely our own. We have been invaded, not merely by alien beings from an alien world coming into our world, but by an alien state of being which has come into our very selves, into our minds. Can we, at this moment, say that we have sovereignty over our own being? Do we have the power of self-determination, the power to shape our own identity? Perhaps we do...for the moment. But while our minds are threatened by the kind of invasion which we have already suffered once, we cannot be sure. We can never be sure, until we have removed that threat.

"The course of action which is forced upon us is not one that we would take lightly. What we have to do now is cause for regret, and sadness, and guilt, and shame. I do not seek to avoid these truths. But we have no choice. In order that we may preserve our selves against destruction—individually and collectively—we must take steps to assure that no such invasion of our being can ever take place again.

"Not long ago, I proposed the establishment of a Second Euchronian Plan, directed toward the reclamation of the Underworld. That Plan has been changed. We now know that there exists in the Underworld a menace to everything that we have, and everything that we are. That menace must be destroyed, and we can take no chances whatsoever in the matter of its destruction.

"I must tell you now that the Euchronian Council has already decided, and plans have already been put in progress, to take the necessary steps, with all attendant precautions.

"All life in the Underworld is to be extirpated. The surface of the ancient Earth is to be absolutely and completely sterilized. This will be accomplished with all possible speed."

52.

The camp was ablaze with light, while the technical staff who had spent so many patient hours setting up the tents and the complex equipment now dismantled and disassembled them again. This time, there was not so much patience about the way they worked, and rather more unseemly haste.

There was little enough opportunity to talk to one another. When they stopped for food and rest they did so in small groups and they took their breaks seriously. For the most part, they had little to say to one another. They had talked themselves to a standstill in the fearful hours following the wave. They were tired men, now, moving like machines, with a permanent haze behind their eyes that was compounded of exhaustion and anxiety.

The exception was Felipe Rath. He wanted to talk. He was no less tired and no less distracted than his companions, but he had something niggling at his mind that he wanted to let out—that he felt compelled to set free. He chose to tell Zuvara, because he felt that Zuvara was likely to understand—and also because Zuvara was peripherally involved, *via* a small sin of omission.

"Harkanter's dead," said Rath.

"I know," said Zuvara. "We all know."

"But I'm partly responsible, in a way. In a way, you are too."

Zuvara stared at him. There was no emotion in his eyes, but with the mask obscuring his features and the strangeness of his manner due to fatigue, Rath fancied that he could see loathing in the stare.

"The other night," Rath explained, hesitantly. "You were...on guard. You must have fallen asleep."

"What has that to do with Harkanter? I don't remember falling asleep."

"You must have. They came into the camp. Joth Magner and...the one that killed him. It was my gun—the one that shot Harkanter. They came right into the camp and took it. You let them in. I let them out. That's what I mean when I say that we helped to kill him. If you hadn't fallen asleep, or let them through behind your back, or whatever...and if I hadn't let them go...."

"They stole your gun," said Zuvara. His voice was faint and monotonous, as though it came from a long distance. "So what? I didn't know that someone was going to steal a gun to kill Harkanter. Neither did you."

"But I did."

"You knew they were going to kill Harkanter?"

"No. But I let them take the gun. I knew they were going after Harkanter, because they wanted to rescue the rat. I could have warned him, but I didn't. I just let them go. I didn't tell anyone. Of course, I didn't know they'd kill Harkanter. How could I? But I didn't warn him. If I had, he wouldn't be dead."

Zuvara felt completely at a loss.

"Why tell me now?" he asked. "What difference does it make?"

"I just wanted to explain," said Rath. "I wanted to explain why I didn't warn him. Magner threatened me, but it wasn't that. He couldn't carry out any threats. But I still didn't warn Harkanter."

"Why?" Zuvara felt compelled to ask.

"Because he didn't have any right. Harkanter. He didn't have any right to go back like that, with the rat, to shout out loud to the whole world that he knew it all. He *didn't* know it all—my pictures proved that. He didn't know anything. So I let them go, to steal his prize specimen, because he didn't have any right.

"But I didn't know they'd kill him."

Rath looked into Zuvara's eyes, to see what he could read there now. But he couldn't read anything. Zuvara wasn't looking at him. In fact, he seemed not to have been listening to Rath at all. He was looking at something over Rath's shoulder—something in the wilderness.

For one brief moment, Rath felt angry. Then the anger died, and the scientist reasserted his will over the tired, self-pitying man.

"I'm sorry," he said. Then he turned.

Joth Magner was walking into the camp. His pace was measured. He was unarmed. His metal eyes—steel globes with horizontal slits, behind which ranged the artificial retinae and the circuitry which filtered and coded the information—searched the masked faces of the men who watched him.

The camp was suspended in a moment of stillness and silence. It was a moment carved right out of time: an encounter utterly strange because it did not involve a meeting of alien worlds or alien minds.

Joth's eyes found Rath, despite the mask, and it was to him that Joth came.

"I'm coming back with you," he said. "It's all done now. All finished."

Rath had to turn away from the stare of the steel eyes.

"It's finished," he agreed.

ABOUT THE AUTHOR

Brian Stableford was born in Yorkshire in 1948. He taught at the University of Reading for several years, but is now a full-time writer. He has written many science-fiction and fantasy novels, including *The Empire of Fear*, *The Werewolves of London*, *Year Zero*, *The Curse of the Coral Bride*, *The Stones of Camelot*, and *Prelude to Eternity*. Collections of his short stories include a long series of *Tales of the Biotech Revolution*, and such idiosyncratic items as *Sheena and Other Gothic Tales* and *The Innsmouth Heritage and Other Sequels*. He has written numerous nonfiction books, including *Scientific Romance in Britain, 1890-1950*; *Glorious Perversity: The Decline and Fall of Literary Decadence*; *Science Fact and Science Fiction: An Encyclopedia*; and *The Devil's Party: A Brief History of Satanic Abuse*. He has contributed hundreds of biographical and critical articles to reference books, and has also translated numerous novels from the French language, including books by Paul Féval, Albert Robida, Maurice Renard, and J. H. Rosny the Elder.